Loykeyaddillybit 2019

THE SHADOW OF OLD LONDON TOWN

Written and illustrated by

Loykey and Lillybit

This edition first published 2010 by
Loykey & Lillybit

This book is a work of fiction. Names characters,
places and incidents are either a product of the
author's imagination or are used fictitiously. Any
resemblance to actual people, living or dead, events
or locales, is entirely coincidental.

A CIP record for this book
is available from the British Library

ISBN 978-0-9562333-2-5

INTRODUCTION

Matt and Molly are twins who were born in Hong Kong. One day their father returns from his office to say they are moving back to England, to old London Town.

A beautiful Victorian town house awaits them there, also the home of the friendly ghost known as *The Shadow* of old London's past.

One day, they are in the attic and they find an old leather book which contains code breakers, clues and an old map of London. Every day becomes an adventure for Matt and Molly as they follow the clues and break the codes, which lead them to their favourite attractions of the past and present in old London town.

This book is an amazing read without a shadow of doubt tap tap tap !!!!!!!

CHAPTERS

CHAPTERS

CHAPTER 1

MOVING TO OLD LONDON TOWN

Matt and Molly are eight year old twins and live in Hong Kong.

One day, their father returned home from his office and said, "I have good news, my work here is complete and my new position is based in London and so we are going back home to England."

Mum was so happy. She had missed her parents and could not wait to return home.

Molly asked, "When do we leave?"

"In four weeks time," Dad replied.

The days went by so quickly and, before they knew it, they were saying goodbye to all the friends they had grown up with.

The cases were packed and were all going back to London by ship, while Mum, Dad, Matt and Molly were going by plane.

The day had arrived and they stood outside and looked back at the apartment with tears in their eyes. Matt and Molly had been born in Hong Kong and now at eight years of age, they were off to London to make new friends.

The journey was long and they all fell asleep. Mum woke them just as they were flying over London. They all looked out of the window and saw a million lights shining bright as if they were saying 'Welcome Home'.

It was late in the evening and Dad had booked them into a hotel for the night. It was down by the Embankment in old London Town. Above the door a sign read 'Welcome to The Royal Horse Guards Hotel.'

The family were shown to their rooms just as Big Ben struck midnight. Mum and Dad said goodnight and said that their new home would be ready to move into the following day.

'WELCOME TO LONDON'

Matt and Molly lay in their beds with the bay windows open, listening to the groaning noises of the city that they had never heard before. They could hear the boats going up and down the River Thames, the fire engine sirens and the aeroplanes coming in to land.

The twins went off to sleep and dreamt of their new home. Would it be old or would it be new, would there be stairs or just one floor? As they slept the bay windows blew shut and not a sound was heard until the next morning, when Mum shouted out, "Breakfast time, rise and shine."

Matt and Molly went downstairs to the breakfast room. The hotel was very busy and full to the brim. There were tables with lovely things to eat on them and they loaded up their plates. They ate it all until they were full. "Now that's what I call a full breakfast," said Matt.

Dad said, "I will settle the bill as our new home awaits." The concierge waved down a taxi for them and off they went down the side of the River Thames. They could see the London Eye, standing so tall with the capsules full of tourists. Mum suggested that it might be a good idea to try that one day.

Mum was so excited to start writing again and said, "I think London is going to give me a lot of new ideas about children living their past dreams."

Dad pointed, "Look, we are nearly there," and in the distance they could see Tower Bridge with its arms up in the air letting a boat through underneath.

Up around the corner they went and the taxi driver said, "Yes, mate, we're here." The driver unloaded their luggage and put it down on the path. Towering above them was the Gherkin, which was a huge office block made of glass and looked like a big Easter Egg.

Dad said, "My new office is in there." Matt and Molly could not believe their eyes, as they stared up at the building with the tinted glass shining bright and not a person in sight.

As they turned they saw a beautiful old Victorian house with steps leading up to the front door. Across the road were Tower Bridge and a view right down the river to Westminster. They all walked up the steps to the front door and Dad put the key in the lock and, as it turned, the door gradually opened and this was where their adventures were about to begin.

CHAPTER 2

THE SHADOW APPEARS

Matt walked in and the others followed into a beautiful hallway with a tiled floor and a large winding staircase leading up to all four floors.

On the left hand side was a Victorian hat stand with a mirror above. There was an old black hat hanging from the hook and a long black cane, with a silver knob on the end, resting in the umbrella stand.

Mum removed the hat and cane from the stand. "They must belong to the previous owners of the house" she said, and dropped them down onto the floor.

Dad said, "They are very old they must be worth something."

Molly walked into the lounge and they all followed. At one end stood a very large fireplace and at the other end was a large bay window overlooking the River Thames.

"I'm going to like it here," Mum said, and everybody agreed.

Molly said, "Let's go and look at the kitchen." It was huge and at one end was a lovely dining area which led into a glass conservatory overlooking the lawn.

Matt said, "I would like to see our bedrooms, please." They all shuffled back into the hallway and, to their amazement, the hat and cane were back on the hat stand. Mum said, "That can't be, Molly, was that you or Matt?"

"No, it wasn't us."

Mum said, "Perhaps we have a ghost?"

Molly shook her head and cried, "I hope not," and ran up the stairs to the first floor.

Dad shouted, "The first floor bedroom is mine and Mum's," as they followed her up the stairs.The second floor had three bedrooms and a bathroom and the third floor had two large bedrooms with bathrooms en suite, one each for Matt and Molly.

Molly shouted to them, "What's behind this door?" and as she opened it there was an old stone staircase. They all followed her up to the roof space. "Oh, Wow," said Molly. It was beautiful with lovely old oak floors and attic windows at each end.

Matt looked out of one of the windows and said, "Look, I can see Big Ben." Molly and her Dad were looking out of the other end and they could see Canary Wharf.

After they had finished looking around, they all went back downstairs and Dad decided to light the fire in the lounge. The previous owners had left an old sofa which they had decided to keep because their furniture was not due to arrive for another two weeks.

Matt and Molly sat gazing into the fire when, all of a sudden, there was a knock at the door. It was the delivery of their new beds.

Molly shouted, "What's for supper?"

Dad replied, "Why don't we all go out and find a nice restaurant to celebrate our move to old London Town?" Everyone agreed that it was a good idea and they went upstairs to get washed and changed.

On their way out Molly looked up and noticed that the old black hat and cane had gone. She never said a word but kept this to herself.

On the other side of Tower Bridge they found a lovely Italian restaurant. The waiter showed them to their table, and Matt said, "Pizza and chips for me," and Molly had the same.

The night sky came in so fast and as Matt glanced out of the window a shadow whizzed past. It looked like a man who had an old black hat and cane just like the ones on the hat stand. Matt rubbed his eyes and the shadow disappeared across the road to Tower Bridge. He did not say a word as he thought his family would think he was mad.

After a lovely dinner, Dad settled the bill and they all walked back across Tower Bridge. Matt suddenly heard a *tap tap tap* sound. They looked round but there was nothing to see. As they walked off the bridge Matt saw a shadow going up the steps to their front door in Nightingale Square. *The Shadow* walked straight through the door. Not a key was used. "It must be a ghost. Molly isn't going to like this," Matt thought.

Off to bed they all went. Matt just lay there thinking about what he had seen. After a while he went to see if Molly was alright. He whispered, "Molly, are you awake?"

Molly replied, "I am now."

Matt said, "I can't sleep, I keep thinking of the old black hat and cane. I never told you earlier but I saw a shadow with the hat and cane just walk straight through our front door, so somewhere in this house I think there is definitely a ghost." They both lay on the bed till they fell asleep dreaming of *The Shadow* they might meet.

CHAPTER 3

THE CODE BREAKER BOOK

The next morning Matt and Molly woke up to the sun shining through the bay window. They were excited about what the day would bring. After getting washed and dressed they went downstairs for breakfast.

In the hallway the old hat and cane were in their usual places and on the hat there was a note pinned to the outside. Matt took it from the hook and read it out. It read, 'Hello, you two, so you know I'm here. I am *The Shadow* of old London Town and I am pleased you are here. I think we will have lots of fun, so watch out for me; I'm everywhere, on this floor and even upstairs behind the attic door. Anyway, for now, have a good day.'

Molly said to Matt, "It sounds like we are going to have fun." They went and sat down and Mum said, "Did you both have a good night's sleep?"

"Yes, thank you," they both said.

Mum had just received a letter in the post from their new school. She told them they would be starting in a couple of weeks, so they had plenty of time to settle into their new home.

Matt and Molly ate their breakfast and Mum said she was going to the study to start work on her new book. Molly said, "What is it called?"

Mum replied, "I don't know. I haven't got a title for it yet. Perhaps I will know later." She shut the door and there she stayed until tea, as she never came out when she was writing a book.

Meanwhile, Matt picked up a note from Dad. It read, 'Gone to my new job not far away in the big Easter Egg, high in the sky.'

Matt and Molly went outside into the garden and there, as Dad said, was the big Easter Egg towering up into the sky. They stood there waving their hands just in case he was looking out, but they could not see a thing as the windows were black tinted glass.

After they had looked in the garden, they went back inside to have a look around. Molly said, "What about starting with the attic?"

"Good idea," said Matt, and off they went.

By the time they reached the attic, they were both out of breath. There were boxes of all shapes and sizes that had been left by previous owners; they both wondered why they had been left behind.

In the corner was an old brown trunk. Matt opened the lid and inside were lots of old books. He picked up a little brown leather book and blew the dust off, which made them both sneeze. On the front cover it read, 'The tales of *The Shadow* of old London Town.' Matt opened the first page and Molly asked "What does it say?"

He read, 'This book is full of clues and code breakers and *The Shadow* will be with you all the way so don't delay. Tonight, at midnight, Big Ben will ring, go downstairs and see what the note of *The Shadow* brings. The code breaker will start and if you are clever, by the time you have finished the book you will have found all the best spooky places in town. Good Luck, and, yes, now you can frown.'

As they sat there they heard the **t**a**p t**a**p t**a**p** of the cane. They looked down the stairs and there on the next floor, was *The Shadow*. He was wearing his hat and carrying his cane. He looked up and they could see that he had no face. He just mumbled, "See you at midnight, and don't be late."

Matt and Molly ran back to their bedrooms. They both lay on their beds thinking what was going to happen. Just at that moment Mum shouted up, "Tea is ready."

After they had eaten, they decided to have an early night as they knew they had to be up for midnight. They lay in their beds and the moon was shining down. Neither of them could sleep but that was just as well because, all of a sudden, Big Ben chimed his bells and it was now time.

Matt and Molly crept downstairs and there, on the hat stand, was a note on the hat. They grabbed it and quickly ran upstairs and a voice down below shouted up, "Don't forget: he who dares, wins!"

The twins went into Molly's bedroom and Matt said, "Quick what does it say?"

She opened the first page and there was a map of old London past. There were fifteen places that had been marked in red with an X. Underneath there was writing which said, 'The clue of what to do, but not to be read until the next morning after breakfast.'

Matt said, "Read it."

"No, we must abide by the rules," Molly replied.

CHAPTER 4

ARMY'S LOST

Matt and Molly awoke very excited. Matt said, "Please can we read the book now?"

"Yes, Matt, I think we have waited long enough."

Molly picked up the book and she slowly read the clues and the code breaker.

ARMY'S LOST

Let's go to see a hero,

Towering above he will be.

I'll see you in the water spray.

Just a shadow you may say.

Catch me, and then we'll dry off

Then you can see what's on my cloth.

It might be silver or it might be gold

But it's definitely very old,

Never to be sold.

PIGEONSILIONSIWATERISKYIARMYS LOST

Matt said, "What does it mean," and just at that moment a piece of paper slid under the door. Matt picked it up and read it out, it said, 'Meet you after breakfast at the front door at ten forty four.'

When they went down to breakfast Mum said, "Dad has gone out to play a round of golf. He has a long way to go as there is no golf club in town. I'm going to be writing all day. What do you two have planned for today?"

Matt and Molly never said a word about their new friend but decided to tell Mum that they were going to feed the birds down by the river. They packed their rucksacks with some cake, fruit and a bottle of water and went to the front door as arranged, when the clock said ten forty four.

As they grabbed their hats and coats Molly noticed that the hat and cane had gone. They opened the front door and there, across the square, he stood.

As they walked down the steps he whizzed past them and shouted, "Come on! The chase has begun, take your time and keep reading the rhyme."

Matt shouted back, "It's easy for you floating along. We've got to run."

Molly read,

'Let's go to see a hero.'

20

Matt replied, "There must be so many heroes in old London Town."

"Yes, but this one is towering high with a water spray."

Matt said, "Let's sit on this bench and have a rest while we try to work it out."

Molly opened the book and asked, "All these words are mixed up! What is all that about?"

Matt replied, "It looks like we are going to get wet, but it must be worth it because there is silver and gold."

Just as they were deep in thought The Shadow stepped out from behind a tree and said, "Come on, back on your feet and run through the crowds." As they followed they started to break the code.   They were walking down the Embankment where there was a sign directing them to Trafalgar Square. All of a sudden, a pigeon flew past and nearly knocked Matt's hat off. Molly shouted, "The PIGEON, that's a part of the code!"

The Shadow shouted, "You could be right, come on we're nearly there!" In the distance they could see Trafalgar Square with hundreds of pigeons everywhere.

On the corner was a fountain with water spraying out, then, from the corner of his eye, Matt noticed a statue. He said, "A lion standing in the spray, this must be a code, **LION, WATER**."

They sat down and opened the book, Molly said, "The code says **SKY**. They both looked up in the air and there, on a tall column, was a large man with one of his arms missing.

"That's it," shouted Molly, "**ARMY's LOST**.

That's the code and the clue. Look, the name at the bottom says Nelson. He's high in the sky, pigeons at his feet, army's lost and lions in the water spray."

"Yes, we've cracked it." said Matt, "Now, where is *The Shadow* and our prize? But remember, we have got to get wet."

Suddenly out from nowhere *The Shadow* came floating past and said, "To get your prize you must touch my cane," and off he went, floating in and out of the water spray.

Matt and Molly followed him until they were wet through. Then Matt grabbed his cane and they all sat down to dry off. *The Shadow* gave them a cloth and, as they dried themselves, two coins fell out. They were two very old silver sixpences. He said, "Keep them safe as one day they could be your saviour. Well done, the first code you have broken, now it's time for home. With *The Shadow* behind, you'll never be alone."

When they arrived home Dad was already back from his round of golf. Matt said, "Hole in one?"

Dad replied, "Yes, the drinks were on me. You look very wet, where have you been?"

Molly said, "We've had a great adventure. We sat down by a fountain which stopped and started and as we looked in, there lay two coins." Dad said, "They're amazing. They could be worth a lot so keep them safe."

Mum shouted out, "It's time for tea and then early to bed as tomorrow we have been invited to friends for tea. We have not seen them for years and their children are the same age as you."

Matt and Molly went up to bed, and Molly said, "It's a lot better here in London than Hong Kong."

There was a knock at the door. Molly opened it but there was nobody there, just the sound of a cane that went **tap tap tap**.

"Goodnight," they both said.

CHAPTER 5

THE LARGEST HOUSE IN TOWN

Molly had been up all night. She had decided to write a diary about their adventures and had gone downstairs to borrow some writing paper from Mum's study. She had written about twenty pages and thought that nobody was going to believe them about their friend the ghost in the house.

There was a **tap tap tap** at the window. Molly went over to have a look. It was *The Shadow*. He was cleaning the windows, and Molly opened the window and asked, "Why?" He wiped over the window and just murmured, "It's better in the dark, without a doubt, because nobody sees me flying about."

The next morning, Molly and Matt went down for breakfast. As they sat there Mum was looking out of the dining room window. She scratched her head and said, "It looks like someone has cleaned all of our windows. Yesterday there were smears everywhere and today not a sign, just clean gleaming glass."

Molly coughed and said, "It must be a shadow of the light."

Mum replied, "No, they have definitely been cleaned." Dad walked into the kitchen and Mum said, "Was it you who cleaned our windows?"

He said, "No, I don't do things like that."

Matt looked at Molly and whispered, "What has happened?"

Molly replied, "It was *The Shadow*. I saw him right in front of my eyes."

Dad said, "As long as there is no bill that will be fine."

After breakfast Mum said, "Right, go and get ready then we will be off to meet our friends."

Matt and Molly were back at the front door in no time and there, next to the hat stand, was an old bucket full of dirty water and a couple of old cleaning rags and a note. Molly bent over and picked it up. "What does it say?" asked Mum.

'I have just cleaned your windows. Don't worry you don't have to pay, not this time anyway.' "Thank goodness," said Dad.

Mum was frowning and looked at Matt and Molly. She started smiling and said, "A little joke you two?" "No, not us!" Matt and Molly just smiled.

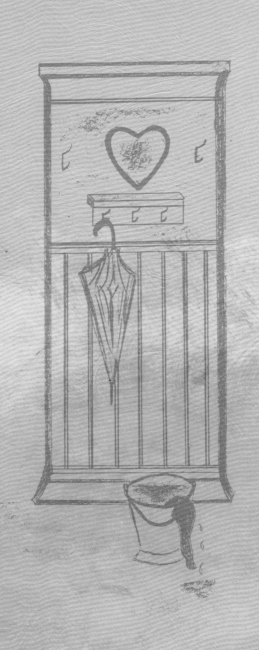

Dad opened the door and off they walked. Mum said, "It's not too far up Petticoat Lane and into Times Square."

As they started their journey, the market traders had just begun to open their stalls. There were men and women shouting, "Get your fruit and veg for a pound." There were watches and toys and rails full of clothes, but Matt and Molly only had their silver sixpences, never to be sold, and so they all just kept walking.

After a while they turned the corner into Times Square. It was quiet and so beautiful with all the birds in the trees. Mum walked up to the front door and rang the bell. A little boy opened it and said, "Hi, I'm Tim and this is my sister Rosie. Please, come in."

The two families were overjoyed to meet again and talked endlessly about old times. The children played games all afternoon and after tea it was time to go. Mum said, "Rosie and Tim must come to stay one weekend." Matt and Molly were excited and thought that would be great, but how would they explain their new friend *The Shadow*?

Everybody said their goodbyes and off they went back home. As they turned into their road Matt and Molly noticed *The Shadow* go up the steps and through the door.

By the time they stepped into the hallway, the hat and cane were back in place.

"I have thrown that hat and cane out so many times and I cannot believe they are back," said Mum. Molly shouted, "I like them there," and Dad agreed. "Yes, I think they make the place look homely. Well kids, I think it is early to bed as your new school waits."

The week at school was very different from Hong Kong but Matt and Molly settled in. Finally, Friday night arrived, there was a **tap tap tap** at Molly's door and it all started once more. The note was left at midnight, just like the week before. They both lay on the bed and read:

THE LARGEST HOUSE IN TOWN

So jump on bus route no. 19

To Trafalgar Square.

The house is at the bottom of the lane

And not the square.

Pigeons will follow you until you are there

But don't get bitten by the dogs or the mares.

When you are there, you'll see a change

So for goodness sake be on your guard

Or you will be locked up on a charge.

LANE/CHANGING/BIG HOUSE/RULER

Matt and Molly awoke after a restless night dreaming of what the clues may mean. They ate their breakfast and told Mum they were going out to play.

The hat and cane had already disappeared and *The Shadow* was nowhere in sight. Molly looked around but there was nothing on the ground, no note, not even a sign. They reached the bus stop and were waiting for No. 19. Suddenly, a big red double decker bus appeared. "All aboard," said the bus conductor. Molly handed him the money and was given two tickets. Then, upstairs they ran, to the front of the bus so they would have the best view.

The bell rang and off the bus went. As the bus turned the corner, Matt and Molly could see St. Paul's Cathedral - a large domed building with steps so high. Matt said to Molly, "Open the book and read the code breaker again. I don't know what it means." They thought and thought and Molly said, "This is going to be harder to crack than the last one."

Before they knew it, they had arrived at their destination and the bus conductor shouted, "All off for Trafalgar Square." As they jumped off the bus they saw Nelson on his column. Molly said, "This is where we ended up last week."

Matt shouted, "Pigeons, look, pigeons everywhere! We should have bought a basket of seed. Never mind, next time."

Matt said, "Look the pigeons are flying towards the archway over in the corner." As they walked they heard a "psst," and as they turned they saw *The Shadow* having a wash in the fountain. He shouted, "How is the code breaker going? I don't think you are there yet. Perhaps down the Mall you should go." Then he disappeared into the spray.

Matt and Molly continued walking and heard an old couple say to each other, "Would you like to walk down the Mall?" Molly said, "Quick, follow them," and off they went through the archway.

In front of them was the most amazing roadway, but with no cars. It looked like a lane. Matt said, "It's in the code, **LANE**. As they reached the end of the Mall a large building appeared with big gates and railings all the way round. Molly said, "Perhaps this is it?"

Matt said, "It is a **BIG HOUSE**, Yes, that is one of the codes."

People started moving nearer the gates and someone shouted out, "Look, it is the changing of the guards." Matt smiled and said "Yes, another code, **CHANGING**." Then, from the right a horseman and guards dressed in large furry hats appeared.

They marched and changed places with each other, one by one.

The man next to them said, "Wow, what a picture, we have now seen the changing of the guards at Buckingham Palace."

Matt said, "We have one more code to break. It says **RULER**. Molly said, "Yes, it is the Queen's house. She is the ruler of the Country. Brilliant! We have cracked the code breaker yet again. I wonder whether there is a prize this time."

At that moment *The Shadow* came floating past and said, "This time the prize is right in front of your eyes, and just at that moment the Queen appeared and started to wave. She saw Matt and Molly and blew them a kiss. Molly said, "Wow, the Queen of England in her big house, nobody is going to believe what she did."

On the way home up the Mall, Molly looked back and instead of the Queen, *The Shadow* took a bow. Matt said, "That was fun. Let's get back for tea. Our job is done."

That night they lay in bed thinking of the big house and was it really the Queen or *The Shadow* in disguise? Suddenly, there was a **tap tap tap** at the door. It was *The Shadow*. He whispered "Goodnight," and just for a joke Matt replied, "Good night, Queenie."

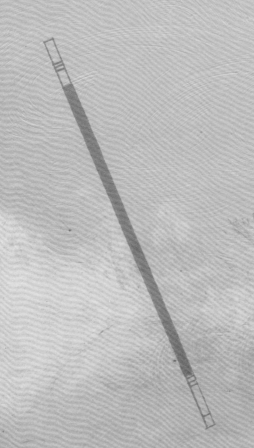

TAP TAP TAP

CHAPTER 6

YOU'LL BE HANGING AROUND

Matt knocked on Molly's door and shouted, "Come on, wake up lazy bones, it's breakfast time."

During breakfast Mum reminded them that it was half term at the end of the week and that Uncle Frank and Aunt Laura were coming to stay for the weekend. "It would be good if we could show them some places of interest while they're here, so perhaps you two could have a think about where they would like to go."

All week Matt and Molly kept thinking, and they both thought that *The Shadow* would be the best bet to give them a treat. So they turned the tables and left him a note asking where they could go.

On Friday night there was a **tap tap tap** at the door. When Molly opened it there was a note on the floor. It read, 'From *The Shadow*,' saying 'Yes, I would like to help. Look at your code book and choose No. 3 and tell your parents and your Aunt and Uncle that their day in London will have lots of codes and clues, so read the book and work it out so that when you leave you know what it's all about.'

Molly ran to Matt's bedroom and said, "Look, **The Shadow** has said in the note our treat for Auntie and Uncle is No. 3 in the book," and with that Molly read it out.

YOU'LL BE HANGING AROUND

It could be on the wall or maybe on the floor.

The entrance is free just walk through the door.

Thousands of people see me and glare.

They think it's their shadow, then stop and stare

But no, they walk away and I'm still there.

The name of this place sounds like mate

But it's not something you put on your plate

So don't hang around like me

As there's plenty more junk to see.

JUNKIFREEISWAYING BRIDGEI FRAMEDILYLE

Matt looked at the book to see where it was on the map but all he could see was a big red X,

so they both decided to wait until the weekend when their adventure would begin.

Saturday arrived and so did Uncle Frank and Aunt Laura. The last time they had seen Matt and Molly, they were both sleeping in cots.

Aunt Laura said, "Look how you have grown," and handed them two presents out of her bag. Matt and Molly ran upstairs to open them.

They had both been given books about old London town, but not a shadow in sight.

"Thank goodness, as we are writing a book ourselves," said Molly.

During dinner that evening Mum said, "Kids, what place have you decided to take us to tomorrow?"

Matt replied, "It's a secret, but here is the plan." He gave each a piece of paper on which there were codes to break. He said, "You must not look at them till morning or you will break the spell."

With that Matt and Molly said they were off to bed and wished them goodnight.

Aunt Laura said, "The kids are just like you, Sis. I think they will be writing just like you very soon."

"Yes, I think you're right, they have a talent like mine," she replied.

The next morning at breakfast Uncle Frank asked, "Can we have a look now?" Molly nodded and said, "O.K."

Aunt Laura scratched her head and studied the piece of paper and said, "It's all a bit of a muddle, I have no idea."

Dad just smiled and said, "It looks like we're going to the shed."

Mum asked Matt to give them a clue. He replied, "We don't know. We found it in an old book. We just have to follow the clues and we will be fine. We must go over to the south side, so Tower Bridge here we come."

Everybody put on their hats and coats as it was a cold, windy morning. Mum looked up and realised the black hat and cane had gone, "At last!" She cried. Matt and Molly just looked at one another and smiled, "He's up to his old tricks. Let's go," Matt whispered.

Half way across Tower Bridge Uncle Frank told everyone to stand still while he took a picture. As he pressed the button, *The Shadow* ran past. Only Matt and Molly saw him, the others thought it was the flash.

Dad asked Molly where they found the book. Molly replied, "We found it up in the attic and it is such fun."

Matt walked down the steps and everyone followed. At the bottom, right in front of them was an ice cream parlour. Mum asked, "Anybody want one?"

and Uncle Frank was first in the queue.

Once everyone had their cones they went and sat on a bench looking down the River Thames. The boats were going up and down. They were all boat taxis taking tourists from one end of town to the other.

Dad suggested they took a ride and everyone thought it was a brilliant idea, so they walked to the next stop. A man shouted, "Quick, it's here." Everyone boarded and off they all went.

The view was amazing; there were buildings that they would not have seen if they were on foot walking down the Embankment. They went under the first bridge then on to the next. Just as they passed under the third bridge someone said, "It's the Millennium Bridge, they called it the swaying bridge." As they passed underneath they looked up and saw it swinging from side to side.

Dad glanced at the code breaker and said, "Look, the SWAYING BRIDGE, it's one of the codes." They all agreed that was one off the list. Molly said, "It can't be far from here." So they all disembarked at the next stop and walked back to the bridge.

Once they were there, Uncle Frank stood up against the wall to have a rest and Molly noticed *The Shadow* standing next to him. Uncle Frank thought it was his shadow but when he jumped, *The Shadow* stood still then disappeared into the wall.

Uncle Frank rubbed his eyes and said, "Is that a clue or just my imagination?"

As they were crossing the bridge everyone could feel it swaying from side to side. When they reached the end they all looked back and Dad shouted, "Look, The Tate."

Molly replied, "What's that?" Mum told them it was a special museum open free to the public.

Aunt Laura said, "**FREE**, it's another code we have broken," and crossed another off their list.

As they stood there, Dad shouted, "Look, **LYLE**. up on the building. It's Tate and Lyle the sugar people. That is another code. We have to go back to find the remaining codes."As they entered the building Molly said, "The place is full of **JUNK**. That's another code. There is only one more left and it says **FRAMED**."

 An hour was spent going from room to room but they could not find the final code. Suddenly, a man announced "The art gallery is now open." Strangely, everybody seemed to be staring at one painting in particular.

Underneath the picture were the words 'You've been framed.' Molly shouted, "Yes, we have the last code, **FRAMED**."

As they all walked away there was a **tap tap tap** on the floor. As they turned, the picture was completely empty and not a shadow in sight.

Mum said, "How can that be?" Uncle Frank said, "Perhaps it's the ghost of Tate and Lyle." Matt just winked at Molly, and Dad replied, "Well, I'm not staying to find out. How about we walk home and get some supper?"

When they arrived back at the house the hat and cane were back. Mum just looked and shook her head. Aunt Laura said, "That was such fun. We would love to do that again one day. Do you know, that would make a great book?"

After supper they went to bed and Molly said to Matt, "There wasn't a prize!"

Matt replied, "No, you're right." Just then there was a knock at the door. Molly opened it and, to their surprise, down on the floor was a large box of chocolates - from *The Shadow,* of course.

CHAPTER 7

THE MONEY POT

At the end of the week *The Shadow* had left them a note, it read: 'Tonight you must break the code but this time you will not have to leave the house, so lie in bed and dream what it might be. It's number seven in the book so have a good look.'

Matt asked, "What does it say?"

Molly sneezed and read the code breaker and the clues.

THE MONEY POT

This place will make your money grow

So say, "Yes and not, no"

It will pay you good interest

So don't delay.

It's better than going out to play

INTERESTING/COINS/KINGS AND QUEENS ARE NOTED/COUNTED

"What does that mean?" wondered Molly. They both decided to write down notes to see what they could come up with in one hour.

Matt suggested they put the notes on the table to work out what clues they had between them, most probably not a lot, as this code breaker had got them on the spot.

Matt and Molly sat there scribbling away and after a while they looked at each other, shook their heads and mumbled, "It says, INTERESTING, so perhaps we shall be finding something we like."

Molly then thought. KINGS AND QUEENS ARE NOTED. "Perhaps a book of some kind?" So she wrote down, History book and INTERESTING perhaps, "Lots to look at and read. COUNTED - could be that the book is in the library. Then there are the COINS. Maybe you have to pay to get into the library." Her mind was all over the place.

Matt was in a right two and eight. He just sat there with a blank page unable to put any of the clues together. By the time the hour was up they had both fallen asleep, Molly stretched upside down on her bed and Matt curled up on the chair.

While they were sleeping The Shadow floated through the door and glanced at what they had written, but nothing to talk about.

He looked at Molly's piece of paper, lots of notes but nothing was right. Then he picked up Matt's blank sheet of paper and rubbed his eyes, so he decided to cast a spell which would make them dream about the codes and work them out.

Matt was dreaming he was in a big forest, he had walked for many a mile and decided to have a rest.

He sat down beside a huge fir tree and mopped his brow. It was very hot and there was no sound.

As he sat there he noticed something shining on the ground. He picked it up. It was half a crown, then he saw another and another. As he scratched away all the leaves, he found more and more until he had so many coins he could not carry them all.

He decided to cover the ground with soil and leaves and then he made a mark on the tree, so he could come back another day.

His pockets were full and off he went back home,through the forest then back into the street.

He turned and looked back and the forest had gone. How could that be? As he walked down the street his pockets split and out fell the coins rolling all over the place.

Just at that moment an old man stopped to help him pick them up. He gave Matt an old leather pouch to put them in and said, "They should be in the bank in an interest account, especially **COINS** which are half crowns. They should all be **COUNTED**."

"What bank do you suggest?" asked Matt. The old man pointed and said, "Look, the Bank of England, over there."

Off Matt went and as he looked around all he could see was a shadow on the ground. Across the road the huge building stood and, as Matt looked up, he noticed a plaque with a coat of arms of the King and Queen, and these were the same ones printed on his five pound note.

Matt took the money into the bank and the lady said, "You will be interested in our account." Matt thanked her as she gave him a book and his receipt.

The Shadow had been inside Matt's head and knew what he had dreamt about. Now, it was Molly's turn to dream.

Molly was dreaming of what the code spelt out and went through the clues one by one. 'Where would **COINS** be **COUNTED**?' she thought, 'Perhaps in a bank. Yes, she was on the right track.' She dreamt she was out shopping with Mum who had just paid for some shoes. The lady at the till said, "Look on your ten pound note the **KING AND QUEEN ARE NOT NOTED**. You will have to take it to the Bank of England and they will replace it with a new one, but only if you are interested."

Molly woke up and shouted, "Matt, wake up I have sorted out the codes and the clues!"

Matt grinned, and said, "So have I." They both looked at their pieces of paper and both had the same words written on them, they said:

THE MONEY POT

It's the nickname for the Bank of England

Down in Square Mile,

The place to save your money

That will make you smile.

Matt said goodnight and went back to his room and they both went back to sleep hoping they were in for a treat, but are they, as *The Shadow* they did not beat?

CHAPTER 8

DARK SIDE OF TOWN

It was Friday night and this time *The Shadow* left a note saying, 'I will leave the code breaker tomorrow night.' Matt said, "That is typical. We have all day Saturday free and nothing to do."

As they were having their breakfast Dad said he was going off to the golf course. Matt and Molly asked if they could go, too, "Even if we play on the golf range." At that moment the phone rang. It was Dad's friend saying he would have to cancel today. "No worries," said Dad. "Matt and Molly can come instead, perhaps next week?"

Just as they were leaving Mum said, "Have a good game and hope you beat Dad."

When they arrived at the golf course Dad paid for them to play and the trolley was Matt's for the day.

They drove to the first tee and Dad took his turn first. Up went the ball and landed in the trees. "Not a good start," shouted Matt.

Molly was next; she swung the club up into the air and as it came down she missed the ball, "Just a practice shot," she said.

With the next swing she hit the ball and it went half way down the fairway. Now, it was Matt's turn. He put his ball on the tee and just as he went to hit the ball there was a **tap tap tap** on his shoulder. As he turned, he saw *The Shadow*. Dad and Molly had walked to the side of the course to wait for him to take his shot. "Hello, mate, I hope I haven't put you off, go on hit it," he whispered. Matt swung his club into the air and down it came, the ball went flying through the air. Dad shouted, "Look, it's landed on the green!" They could not believe it.

Dad took his turn again and it took him two shots to get out of the woods and onto the green. Molly took her second shot and she landed on the green. Off they went towards the green and they saw that Matt's ball was only one foot away from the hole, so Dad said, "You go first, Matt," and he putted it straight in. At that moment a voice over his shoulder said, "You are going to win." He looked around, but nobody was there, just his shadow on the ground.

Off they went round the course until they arrived at the last hole. Their balls were all on the green, and Dad's was half a metre away from the hole. Dad said, "Molly, you go first." She tapped her ball across the green and it went straight in.

Now it was Matt's turn. He hit his ball and it went straight for the hole. It rolled round the top of the hole three times before it dropped in.

Finally it was Dad's shot. He tapped the ball and it went straight over the hole. He tried the shot again and missed a second time, so he took a deep breath and gently putted it in the hole.

Dad suggested a glass of lemonade in the club house while they added up the score cards to see who had won. Molly said, "I have scored forty-eight."

Matt quickly added up his, and it totalled thirty-seven. Dad's face went bright red, "I don't believe it. I have scored thirty-eight, so, Matt, you are the winner by one point."

Matt thought, 'Just as *The Shadow* had said.'

When they arrived home Mum asked them, "How was your game?"

Dad shook his head, and announced that Matt had won by one point, they had both played very well and they all had a wonderful day.

Mum told them to sit up as dinner was ready and jokingly said, "Let's hope Dad's defeat won't spoil his appetite!"

"No, definitely not, but I must practice before I take them out again."

After dinner Matt and Molly said, "Thank you, Dad, for a lovely day at the golf club."

Matt and Molly said goodnight and went up to bed to read their books.

As Molly lay there, she heard a voice out on the stairs, she opened the door and there, on the landing, was *The Shadow*. He turned and said, "Tomorrow you could lose your head, so look at code eight in your book." She ran to Matt's room and said, "Quick, open the book to code eight. It's where we will be going tomorrow."

DARK SIDE OF TOWN

If you find this place,

It's possibly underground

But don't make a sound.

The man at the top of the stairs,

He will let you in

But only when you pay him half a crown

Then he will let you down.

It's up to you to get back to the top

But only when you've had a shock

SOUTHSIDE/BARS/KEYS/SCREAMING/ DARK/CHAINS

On Sunday morning they both got up extra early and went down for breakfast. Mum asked them what they were doing today. "Don't tell me, you're going to feed the birds and read your books?"

"Yes," they both replied.

As they were going out the front door Mum shouted out, "I've got a box of rubbish to go out."On the top was the hat and cane. "Oh, no," Molly said, and as they put the box out by the bins, a flash of light came past, "Oh, no you don't," a voice said and it was *The Shadow*. He picked up the hat and cane and mumbled, "Let's go and play the game."

Matt and Molly quickly followed him across Tower Bridge to the South side. Matt said, "That is one of the codes - SOUTHSIDE." They carried on running after him but he was gone. They walked along the side of the Embankment and after a while they decided to have a rest.

Matt and Molly sat on a wall and there, in front of them, was *H.M.S. Belfast*. It was a big warship that is now a museum. Matt got his camera out and took some pictures of the ship. The guns were enormous. As they walked along further there was a sign saying '£5 to go on board to look around,' but neither of them had any money.

Before they knew it, they were standing in a long queue and the man on the ship shouted, "O.K., come on board." Matt and Molly were pushed with the crowd, when Matt was just about to say they had no money, the man said, "Welcome aboard."

They were with a coach-load of northerners, but Matt whispered, "Don't say a word as our voices will stand out as we are from the south."

Matt and Molly walked around the ship inside and out, and then the captain of the ship announced that dinner was served. They both said, "That sounds just fine." Both of them ate their dinner without a word. Before they left a man gave them a carrier bag full of souvenirs.

Once they were back on shore they looked inside the bag. There were posters, pens, badges, all the small gifts that were on the ship. "That was good, neither a penny nor a half crown spent," said Molly.

They carried on walking along the Embankment, as it was such a beautiful day, and as they turned the corner there was another old ship. The sign on its hull read *The Golden Hind*. It was a tall ship with large sails. Matt got his camera out and clicked away like mad. Matt and Molly could only stand and admire this ship as it was so old nobody was allowed on board.

Suddenly, they heard a tap tap tap and as they turned, there stood *The Shadow* with his cane, then, off he went again. He shouted to them, "Not far now, listen for the CHAINS." All of a sudden, Matt and Molly were in a dark tunnel that smelt damp and felt very spooky. It made them run back out into the daylight again.

Matt said, "Quick, look at the book and see what the codes say." "We are nearly there, and we must listen for the chains," *The Shadow* said, but they could not hear a sound.

As they walked they heard people screaming, "This must be the place," Molly said. At the top of the stairs there was a man dressed in old rags who said, "Do not worry about the skeleton in the cage. He's very friendly! Come on down, children, I will waive the half crown." So down Matt and Molly went.

It was very D**ARK**, Molly went cold and murmured, "That's one of the codes." Matt and Molly went down an old stone staircase; it was damp and very slippery. When they got to the bottom of the steps the screaming noises were scaring Molly. Then, in the corner they could see a prison cell with B**ARS**, Matt said, "Another code."

As they turned they could see C**HAIN**s on the wall and a set of K**EYS**. Molly said, "Stop, Matt, they are the other two codes. Now, please can we get out of here?" Matt put his arm round Molly while

The Shadow placed a hand on Matt's shoulder and whispered in his ear, "It's not worth half a crown to come down here."

Before they knew it they were back at the top of the staircase. Matt and Molly thanked the man, who said, "Come back soon and bring *The Shadow*."

As the old man crept back down the stairs he muttered, "He is a good friend and stays all night sometimes. I don't know who gives me the most frights - our friend or the skeletons in the cells."

Just as the old man disappeared at the bottom of the stairs they heard him shout out one more time, "Thank you for coming to

THE DARK SIDE OF TOWN."

As Matt and Molly walked away Molly said, "I didn't like that place. That's for robbers and murderers but not for us." Matt said, "Listen, Molly." They could both hear people screaming but not from Clink Jail. They followed the noise and there, in front of them were The London Dungeons. Molly said, "This is definitely the dark side of town."

At that moment *The Shadow* drifted past and called out to them, "You have won again; perhaps you are both getting too good for me!" Matt laughed, he said, "What about our prize?"

"Your prize will slip under your door at ten forty-four, so don't fall asleep."Matt and Molly went to bed extra early and sat there reading their books waiting for their prize to arrive. Just as Big Ben struck ten forty-five Molly announced, "He's late." Suddenly, an envelope was slipped under the door. Written on the front was 'Delivered at ten-forty-four.' It also read, 'The rubber seal on this envelope can only be opened when you have cracked this extra code to win your prize for you and your Mum and Dad:'

Look up into the sky

And you will see them high.

Think of the stars

But it's not the Moon or Mars,

Where films are made in the U.S.A.

The red carpet comes out for the stars to play.'

Matt looked out of the window and up into the sky, "Look, Molly, the Moon, the stars and planet Mars." Then they were both thinking of what the films could be, and they both realised at the same moment, "It's Planet Hollywood in Leicester Square, Wow." They opened the seal on the envelope and there inside was a family ticket for food and drink in one of London's favourite restaurants.

Matt went back to his bedroom and he saw

The Shadow in a heap resting on the window seat. Matt said, "Thank you for our treat."

CHAPTER 9

WHAT A SHOW

The weekend arrived quickly and on the Friday night, as Molly lay in her bed, there was a knock on the door. She opened it but there was nobody there. Molly went to Matt's room and asked him if he had seen *The Shadow*. "No," he replied, "I didn't hear a sound."

Molly went back to her bedroom and, on the way, tripped over an old boot. It had a note inside so she picked it up and went back to Matt's room and they both sat and read it out together.

WHAT A SHOW

Take a long walk on the north side of the river,

Touch the mime

And it will take you back in time.

It's a show which might catch you

If you are slow

So off to theatre land you must go

But hurry before the curtain call

Or you will see nothing at all.

CHEESE/MIME/APPLAUSE/BACK IN TIME/TRAP

Molly said goodnight to Matt and, before going back to her room, she went downstairs for a glass of milk. On the stairs she saw *The Shadow* lying in the window seat. She whispered to him, "Saturday is fine, but after we have fed the birds."

The Shadow replied, "I will help you if you like."

"Yes, please," answered Molly.

The next morning they dressed and told Mum they were off to feed the birds and finish their homework.

Matt and Molly took their basket full of seed and went and sat on the bench next to the River Thames. Out came a pencil and card and on this they wrote, 'FEED THE BIRDS 50p A BAG.'

As soon as they put the sign out, an old lady and gentleman said, "Two bags of seed, please." They handed them a pound coin. Then, out of the blue, came a coach-load of Chinese people. They were following *The Shadow*. He shouted to Matt and Molly, "Quick! Shout out, 'Feed the birds for only 50p a bag.'" Before they could count to ten every bag of seed had been sold. The pigeons had a whale of a time. They had eaten so much food, they just sat there and could not move.

The Shadow floated off shouting, "Now, can we get on with solving the code breaker?"

Matt and Molly followed *The Shadow* down the north side of the Embankment. Matt said, "How much money do you think we made?"

Molly replied, "Ten pounds I think, but it could be more as some of the Chinese people had no change and just threw in a pound coin instead of 50p."

"Brilliant, we will have to do that again," replied Matt.

Suddenly, their pace quickened and they were running trying to keep up with *The Shadow*. Before they knew it, they had followed him all the way to Covent Garden. The place was buzzing and they were very tired. There were dozens of stalls with people selling their wares. So they sat down on a couple of their chairs.

As they sat there looking through the crowds, they could hear people clapping and shouting, "More!"

Matt and Molly went to find out what it was all about. As they squeezed through to the front of the crowd, there was a man dressed up in a suit and wearing a bowler hat. He was completely still, only moving when people dropped money into his hat. His face was white with staring eyes. He moved so slowly. Just then, a lady standing by said, "That's the best mime I have ever seen." She went over and chucked 50p into his hat.

"That's one of the codes, **MIME**." announced Matt. "We have got to touch him and then we will go back in time."

Molly and Matt stepped forward and put a pound into his hat. The man brought his hand down and patted them on the head, and, with a flash of light, they found themselves in a different time. All the children were dressed in shorts and very funny caps. As they looked around, the mime artist had gone and turned into a policeman who was shouting, "Get out of here! Children should not be here." Matt and Molly ran until they were out of breath.

People everywhere were dressed in colourful suits and big furry boots. On the side of an old double decker bus was a poster saying, 'Flower Power for all,' They had gone back in time to 1960.

Just as Matt and Molly were walking along they saw a wooden sign saying, 'Theatre land straight ahead, but watch your head.' Molly said, "Perhaps that's the catch, but I don't think so." As they turned the corner Matt said, "Look, *The Mouse* **Trap**. It's one of the codes, but where does the mouse come into it?" Molly squeaked, "It must be the place, as mice eat cheese and that would be on the mouse trap. As they reached the front door *The Shadow* floated past and said to the ticket man, "There are three of us, my friends and I."

THEATRE

TOKENS

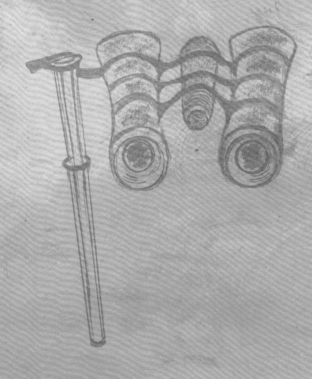

The man said to them, "*The Mouse Trap* will keep you in suspense." By the end of the show all three of them had fallen asleep but were woken up at the end by the **aPplause**, which gave them the last code.

As they left the theatre, Matt asked, "Well, who did it?" Molly looked at him and said, "No idea! I was fast asleep."

Matt said, "I think it was the mouse trap or it could have been the poisoned cheese. What a show, not a penny spent!"

The doorman shouted, "Don't forget *The Shadow*." As they looked back they saw him going round and round in the revolving door. Molly cried with laugher and said, "Why don't you just walk straight through like you do at home?"

The Shadow replied, "I would, but my cloak is stuck around the handle!" With that, Matt and Molly went to help him. They spun round the door and landed on the ground and when they stood up, they were back in their own time. On the way back home, all they could talk about was *The Mouse Trap*.

When they arrived home, Mum asked, "How was your day?" Matt was just about to reply, when Molly kicked him, so he said they had been to Buckingham Palace to see the Queen.

Mum replied, "Oh yes, in one of your dreams!"

71

On their way upstairs Matt said, "That hurt Molly,"

"It was supposed to, it was a trap for you."

Matt said, "Next time I would like you to mime it."

"Very funny," replied Molly.

After supper Matt and Molly said to each other,

"What a week! It's back to school tomorrow."

Matt said, "Wait a minute. We didn't get a prize," and just at that moment a mouse trap appeared on the stairs. *The Shadow* popped his head around the corner and said, "I know it is a bit cheesy, but it is your prize!"

Molly picked it up and as she did four theatre tickets for *The Lion King* fell to the floor. Matt and Molly thanked him and just roared!

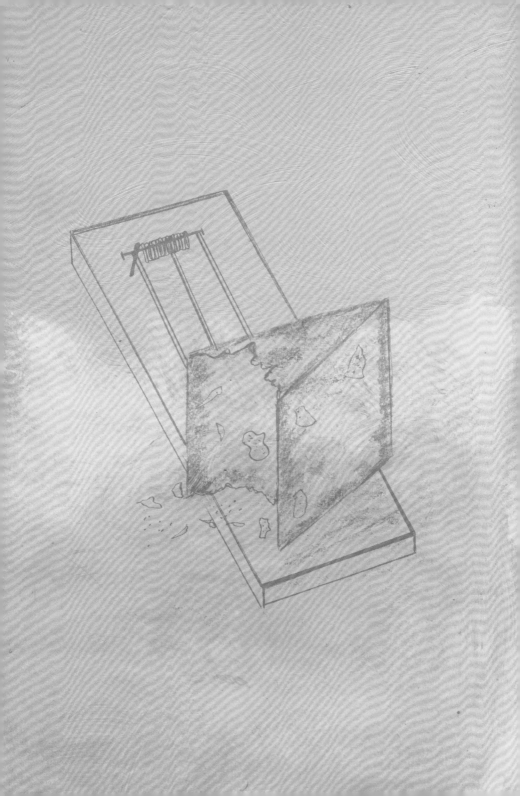

CHAPTER 10

CLOWNS WILL FLY

Matt and Molly were on their way home from school when they saw The Shadow playing games with other children in the square. They could not see him, only his shadow on the ground. As Matt and Molly walked past he said to them, "Would you like to play some games?"

"Perhaps, after we have finished our homework."

Two hours later the twins were still hard at work when The Shadow floated through the door and into Molly's room. "I'm sorry," she said, "We have got so much work to complete, we shall have to play games another day, but while you're here can you tell us what the code breaker is this week?"

The Shadow replied, "It is code no. 10 in the book and just to tease, you will have to dress in cool cotton tops."

All week they thought about what The Shadow had said. Every time they went to ask him for more clues he was out. Matt said to Molly, "He only said cool cotton, so what does that mean?"

Friday night arrived and a note was slipped under the door. Molly picked it up and handed it to Matt and told him it was his turn to read it out.

CLOWNS WILL FLY

It's on the south side of the River.
Watch you don't slide.
It's definitely not there
So you must take care
And when you go back in time
You won't have to touch the mime.
With your cotton tops you will be cool
And don't forget to act the fool

GLASS HOUSE/COTTON/FUN/ROLLER FRIGHT/ANIMALS

Again they both looked puzzled and could not understand the words. "It's definitely not there." Molly said, "It has to be there!"

"No, not if we go back in time," replied Matt.

"So you are saying that it is not there now?"

"Yes, I think so, if that makes sense." The morning had arrived and Mum was busy with her book and shouted out, "Have a good day and think where you would both like to go with Dad and me tomorrow."

"O.K., Mum. See you later." Matt and Molly grabbed the code breaker book and off they went in their cool cotton shirts, just as *The Shadow* had instructed.

Matt and Molly ran across Tower Bridge and down the south side of the Embankment. After a while Molly gasped, "Oh, no, this is the way to Clink Prison," and there, in front of them, was the skeleton in the cage. They quickly ran past and a voice shouted out, "Aren't you coming inside?"

Matt replied, "No, we saw enough last time, thank you very much!"

Every building seemed to get bigger and bigger and there was one that stood out from all the rest. It was glass from top to bottom. Then Matt said, "Look, Molly, the sign above the door, it says Cotton House."

Molly replied, "But it is a glass house."

"That's it. COTTON and GLASS HOUSE, they're two of the codes, how easy was that," Matt replied.

As they walked up towards the big glass doors they automatically opened and there, just inside, *The Shadow* appeared saying, "We have to go back in time." He spun them in the air and as they fell to the ground they opened their eyes, and, to their surprise, they were back in 1955. The building had turned into a magical circus and funfair.

As they went through the entrance, the roller coaster started to move. "That's one of the codes, **ROLLER**," screamed Molly. As it went past they both jumped on. Up and up it went and then down. It took their breath away and Molly started to scream. When the ride had finished they both jumped off and fell to the ground. It had made them light headed. "I'd like to do that again," suggested Matt.

Molly shook her head and said, "I'd rather keep my feet firmly on the ground. You will have to go it alone."

Just then, some clowns shouted, "Don't miss the show." So off they went to the big tent. Matt and Molly sat in the arena. The place was packed and the children were shouting, "We want to see the clowns!" Just then, from the corner of the arena, an old crock car roared in, with hooters beeping and the exhaust pipe back-firing and sounding like cannons. As the old crock shuddered to a halt, the doors fell off and the clowns fell out. The clowns were throwing flour bags and water bombs.

Next on were the flame throwers, not to be attempted by anyone else. It was very clever but not a nice smell.

The **ANIMALS** were on next. Matt said, "Molly, that's one of the codes."

The circus master said, "Now, for the monkeys. They will be having **FUN** chucking currant buns." Matt said, "Yes that's code five. Only one more to go."

The circus master said, "Now, look up above," and everyone gasped. There were six men and ladies standing on platforms sixty feet above the ground with a wire rope tied from side to side. The first one walked across the wire and it started to spring up and down. It was a scary sight and they all took their turn one by one. All of a sudden, they gave everyone a **FRIGHT** as they slid down the ropes and everyone applauded. Matt said, "That's the last code."

After the show Matt and Molly walked outside to the funfair and decided that the dodgems were next.

As they climbed into the car, *The Shadow* jumped in too and said, "Isn't it great?"

"Yes, we wish we could stay here forever," they replied.

Molly said, "No, we can't. But for now, let's have some fun."

As they got off the dodgems Matt realised that they had not paid a penny for any of the rides and the funfair people were charging everyone else except them. *The Shadow* said, "They cannot see you as you're from a different time.

Matt picked up a toffee apple and nothing was said. Then hot dogs were next and then, on the way out,

an ice cream. It was amazing; it was the best time they had ever had.

When they got back to the entrance Matt thanked the man, and Molly whispered, "He can't see us," but the man said, "Hope you've had a good time. We would love to see you again."

Matt and Molly thought, 'How could that be? Nobody was able to see them.' As they walked out of the building, it suddenly turned back to glass, and Matt said, "Thank you, Cotton House, for a lovely day. We hope to see you another time even if we have to pay."

When they arrived home, Mum and Dad asked if they had a good day and they both replied, "Yes, it was pretty fair."

COTTON HOUSE

CHAPTER 11

FACE TO FACE

The next morning, Mum told them, "There's no school on Friday as it's an inset day."

Matt giggled, "Only bugs can go to school."

Molly said, "Don't be a fool. It's a teacher training day."

Mum told Matt and Molly that the chimney sweep was coming and it would be interesting to watch.

That night, Matt and Molly told *The Shadow*. He replied, "That's good because the chimneys are due for a good sweep. I went up the lounge chimney the other week and got covered in soot."

On Thursday evening, *The Shadow* was fast asleep as they walked past the window seat. He suddenly woke up and went, "Psst. Don't forget the chimney sweep is coming tomorrow. He might not be what he seems, so both of you have sweet dreams."

Friday morning arrived and, after breakfast, Mum said she was going into the garden to continue writing her book as it was a beautiful sunny day. She said, "Give me a shout when the chimney sweep arrives. He said he will be here at 10.44."

Matt and Molly sat at the dining table playing a card game called Happy Families when someone knocked at the door.

Matt looked out of the window and said, "It's the chimney sweep."

Molly said, "Mum's in her chair fast asleep," and so Matt answered the door. Matt opened the door and the man said, "Hello, I'm Billy the sweep and this is my mate, Willy."

Out on the pavement was his barrow with his name on the side. He walked in with brushes in his hand and Willy carried a clean sheet. Matt and Molly showed him the lounge fireplace and, to their amazement, Willie went up the chimney, then Billy handed him the brush and the rods. He screwed them together then up and down they went; black soot fell down with every push until the brushes reached the top and popped out of the chimney onto the rooftop.

After the lounge, the sweeps cleaned all the other fireplaces in the house. Once they had finished, they came back down to the hallway and Billy the sweep told them the work was all completed.

Willy, the young boy, was the same age as Matt and Molly but had already been working since he was seven. He was covered in soot from head to toe.

Molly looked out of the window and saw that Mum was still fast asleep but she had left some money in an envelope for the sweep. Billy opened it up and said, "That's not right, this is too much money." And gave them back a £10 note and thanked them. He wrote, 'Paid in full' and signed his name and dated it 1908.

As Matt and Molly watched Billy and Willy walk down the steps, they could see horses and carriages everywhere on the square and realised they had gone back in time yet again. Just as Billy the sweep disappeared out of sight, the whole square turned back to their time.

As Matt shut the door Mum walked into the hallway and looked at the clock and said, "The chimney sweep is late." Molly told her, "No, he has been already and his mate. He has cleaned all the chimneys and left a signed receipt, and you have got some change."

Mum replied, "That's funny. That is not his name. It's Mr. Black and I left him the correct money, he must have made a mistake."

At that moment the doorbell rang, Mum opened it and there stood a tall man wearing a large black hat who said, "Good morning, I'm Mr. Black the sweep. I'm sorry I am late but I had trouble at number eight." Mum said, "I'm very sorry but we are now O.K., but here is £10 for your trouble," and Mr.

Black thanked her and went on his way.

Mum said, "That is weird, how can that be?"

Matt replied, "Perhaps we have dreamt it but I think you will find the job has been done just fine."

Mum said, "Next time, you must call me when someone is at the door," and, as she turned, the old black hat and cane fell off the stand and onto the floor, leaving a dusting of soot all around the mat.

Mum picked up the hat and cane, brushed them off and hung them back up on the stand.

As Matt and Molly went up the stairs *The Shadow* whispered, "I'm very pleased with my new clean hat and also it will be much easier to go up and down the chimneys without sneezing and smelling of soot now that Billy has cleaned them."

Matt asked him what the code was for tomorrow, and *The Shadow* replied, "I can leave you with a little clue. You will be seeing double, but they will not move."

Matt and Molly went off thinking what this could mean. Matt thought, "Perhaps we will be wearing old spectacles and be stuck in a lift?"

Molly said, "Perhaps we will see baby twins strapped in their pram? Anyway we will have to wait till 10.44."

After tea Mum suggested a game of Scrabble. Matt and Molly nodded and said, "Yes, please."

At that moment Dad came home from work and said, "What a day! All our shares have doubled."

Matt scratched his head and said, "What do you mean?"

Dad replied, "Well, instead of staying still the shares have gone up making them more valuable. Some day you will understand and yes, I would love a game of Scrabble."

Mum put the board on the table and Matt picked out the letter A so he went first. He looked at his letters and he made up the word BREAK and got double points. Molly took her turn and put E and R on the end, which made BREAKER. It was Mum's go, and she laid her letters above the E which spelt CODE. Matt looked at Molly and just winked. Finally, it was Dad's turn and he placed his letters which made the next word FACE. It was as if the *The Shadow* was using the words from the code breaker book! The game carried on. Then Dad laid his last letter and won the game.

Mum suggested an early night and Dad agreed as he had to go into work early to count his money. Everyone said good night and off they went to bed.

Molly thought they could read a book until 10.44p.m. and went downstairs to Mum's study. She brought back a book called, *The Candle Wax Dolls*. It was about two young children who lived in a

cottage in the woods and every night, when they went to bed, they would lie looking at the candles flickering in the moonlight, and then, as they slept the candles were blown out by their Mum and during the night, they would turn into wax dolls and have adventures.

At 10.44p.m. a note was slipped under the door and it read:

'Tomorrow, you must stay on the north side and follow your Dad to work because his office will be *en route* for the code of the day.'

FACE TO FACE

Face to face there are celebrities in this place.
The name is very French
But this is only a clue. Whatever you do
Don't get hot or you will melt the lot
And don't let them get on your wick.
Remember your camera and give them a click

STILL/FACE TO FACE/WAX/ A FRENCH LADY

The next morning after breakfast, Dad said, "I'm off to work."

Matt and Molly asked, "Can we come for a walk and see the big egg?"

"Of course," replied Dad and off they all went.

Down the lane and three more streets later, they turned the corner and there was Dad's office towering above. He said, "Have a good day, kids," and they replied, "You, too," and they went on their way. As they were walking, Matt pulled out the map and had a good look. All of a sudden, there was a gust of wind and the map flew up in the air and *The Shadow* caught it and shouted, "It could be a museum, but you will never know." He passed them the map and Molly said, "Look, the British Museum," and off they went. After a while they stopped at a bus stop and decided to catch the next bus to save their feet.

The bus arrived; they jumped on and ran upstairs. The bus conductor followed them up and asked them where they would like to go. They both replied, "Oxford Street by the British Museum, please." "O.K., that will be eighty pence each, please."

Molly looked at Matt and asked him if he had any money. Matt shook his head and said, "No, I have nothing."

Just at that moment there was a gust of wind and

a five pound note floated through an open window. Matt grabbed it quickly and said, "There you go."

The bus conductor said with disbelief, "That was lucky," and took for two fares. As they sat and looked out of the window there, in front of them, was *The Shadow* waiting at the traffic lights on a push bike. He looked up and nodded his head, then the lights changed and off he sped.

Ding Ding went the bell and the bus conductor said, "The next stop is Oxford Street." As the bus came to a halt, Matt and Molly jumped off and there, across the road, was the British Museum. They walked up the steps into the entrance and, yet again, there was no charge: it was free to get in. Once they were inside, they looked all around but not a code was to be found.

Matt and Molly decided to go outside and sit on the steps. As they sat there a man with a hot dog trolley walked past shouting, "Hot dogs, £2 each!" Matt said, "Yes, please. Make that two." Molly took the change left from the five pound note out of her pocket but only had £3.40. Molly said to the man, "May we have a smaller one as we are sixty pence short?"

"That's O.K., I'm feeling lucky as I have just won a bet on a horse called Madam Toy," replied the man.

"Thank you," they both said as they were squeezing tomato sauce over their hot dogs.

After they had eaten they looked at the old map. Molly said, "Look, Pollock's Toy Museum. Come on, Matt, let's go and have a look."

So, off they trotted across Bedford Square and up the road to Goodge Street, and there it was - the toy museum. Matt said, "This must be the place," and, once again, they got in free.

The toys from the past were incredible: there was Humpty Dumpty and his wall; Bill and Ben and Little Weed; on the opposite side there sat Jack Horner and his plum, and the Wombles one, two, and three. They thought hard about the code breaker but there was not a wick in sight, although they were all keeping very still.

Matt and Molly finally decided they must be looking in the wrong place, then with a flash *The Shadow* appeared and said, "Look, it's Sooty and Sweep! But, yes, you're right, you're not there yet but you are very close, It's only a few more streets."

So off they went back into the street and carried on walking. Just then, a double decker bus went past and on the side was a poster which advertised,

Madame Tussaud's. Molly shouted, "That's it, the first code, FRENCH LADY. a madame! We must follow the bus." As they went round the corner the bus had stopped right next to Madame Tussaud's.

There was a queue of people and they decided to stand with them. A voice said, "Doors are now open." As Matt and Molly marched in, they realised they had done it again, they were with a coach-load of students.

The tour guide said, "When you are walking round, the wax works are very **STILL**, or can you catch them out and spot them moving?"

Molly said, "That's the second code."

As they went through the main door the first person they saw was Prince Charles and his dog, and Molly looked at him **FACE TO FACE**.

Matt realised it was another code. Next, were David Beckham and his Posh Spice and round the corner were Doctor Who and his Tardis. At the top of the stairs they could see Harry Potter Just across the way was Billy the Kid and his horse but their favourite of all was *The Shadow*, of course. He was down in the dungeons.

"Hello, what is our prize now we have found all the codes?" Molly asked. He never moved nor made a sound and then Matt touched him and said, "Wow, he's made from **WAX**! Of course, that is the last code." Just then they heard *The Shadow* laugh and he floated from behind a pillar and looked face to face at his wax impression, and said, "Not bad, I'm glad they have caught my good side."

The Shadow said, "Right, it is time to go. It has been fun and the place is going to close. Unless you would like to stay all night, you had better make your way up to daylight."

When Matt and Molly were back in the street Molly said, "I can't walk any more. It is a long way home." At that moment a taxi pulled up beside them and *The Shadow* opened the door. The taxi driver said, "Where do you want to go?"

Matt replied, "Nightingale Square, the other side of town, please."

On the way, Matt and Molly were arguing as they had no money so how were they going to pay? Before they knew it they had arrived home and the taxi driver opened the door and he said, "I heard what you were whispering about and it is your lucky day because it was on my way home." They both said thank you. *The Shadow* said, "That was lucky, but remember, the code breakers will always help you especially when you are stuck and don't know what to do, but don't forget, I am always with you."

When they got in, they told their Mum that they had been to see the celebrities and the stars and Mum replied, "Oh yes, and we're going to have tea on Mars."

"Yes, please," they both replied.

CHAPTER 12

BITS AND PIECES

On Sunday morning when Matt and Molly woke up Molly had decided that she was going to write the next chapter of their book and said, "Matt, you are so far behind with the pictures you will need all day to catch up!"

"O.K.," replied Matt and nodded his head.

After breakfast Molly went to the snug and curled up on the old sofa and started writing.

Matt thought he would draw the pictures later but now he decided he would go up into the attic to have a good look around.

He climbed the old stone staircase and when he got to the top, he found a stack of old books that the previous owners had left behind. He took one of the books, sat down and leant against the wall. As he did, the panel behind him swung round making him fall and as he stood up he could see a little room to the side of the chimney breast. He looked inside and there, in the dark, was a pair of eyes. He took a couple of steps back and just then a bat flew past him and went straight out of the attic window.

When Matt looked back in the little room he could see a battered old tin. As he pulled it out he could see it was painted in many different colours. He opened the lid and inside were three boxes. He took the first one out. It was bright red and inside was an old leather pouch. He pulled the cord and out fell lots of colourful marbles. They were all different sizes but one stood out. It was the largest of them all with every shade of green. Then, out of the pouch fell a note that read:

'He who holds these marbles will roll along through life

And have the good luck of old London town

But when you leave, put them back where they were found!'

The next little box was green and inside was a game called Tiddlywinks. The rules said,

'Flick if you dare, but always only in the can'

The next game was on an old London map dated 1886. On the map was written:

'Hop Scotch is the name of the game

Chalk the floor as the picture says

Then with friends throw the dice

And then hop and scotch

Until you finish the game'

Matt put them back in the old tin and went downstairs to show Molly. "Wow," she said, "can we go out into the street and play?" "Yes," replied Matt.

The first game was Hop Scotch and Matt and Molly found some chalk, but before they had marked out the game, the children from next door asked if they might score.

Molly said, "Yes, and you may play."

It was such fun. The next game was marbles.

Matt rolled the large green one then the others took their turn and tried to hit it but Matt won the game every time.

Next came Tiddlywinks. That was a lot harder, trying to get the small counters into the can. They played all afternoon until Mum shouted, "It's time to come in for tea, and don't forget to bring in your new games."

The only one they left behind was the Hop Scotch as that was just chalk left behind on the pavement.

That night, when they went to bed, Molly said to Matt, "Come and have a look out of the window."

They looked out and saw *The Shadow* hopping, one, two, three, six and falling over his cane. It was so funny watching *The Shadow* trying to play the game of Hop Scotch. "Perhaps next time he would be better with Tiddlywinks in the can,"

Molly said, "Good night, it's back to school tomorrow!" Matt shook his head and replied, "Oh, no."

When Matt and Molly arrived at school, their English teacher said, "Today, children, I would like you all to write a story about a day you have all enjoyed."

Molly sat there and thought of *The Shadow* and then decided she couldn't write about him as nobody would believe her anyway, so she decided to write, about their first day at school in Hong Kong.

In Hong Kong Matt and Molly could not understand a word until they had learnt about spelling with pictures. For instance, butterflies meant love and be kind and the candle was for a guided life. Their time at school there was very different from England and she wrote about her friends, who they nicknamed Ying and Yang. Many a day was spent on the old boats and walking through the food markets.

At the end of the day the teacher told them to leave their stories on their desks. Matt asked Molly, "What did you write about?"

"Our first day at school in Hong Kong," she replied.

Matt said, "That's strange, so did I."

That night, there was a **tap tap tap** at Matt's door and there, on the floor, was a map He picked it up and it flipped open into a scroll with a lace ribbon attached. He went to Molly's room and said, "Look what *The Shadow* has left for us."

He opened it out; it was very dusty and very old. It was a map of old London town. It was all of old buildings and not a new one in sight. No Tate, no Egg, no new office blocks and no London Eye. On the bottom the date read 1840. Molly said, "Look at the name of the streets. I like Pudding Lane and there is Windmill Street, that must be very windy. Then there is Apple Tree Yard."

Matt said, "Look, best of all there is Scotland Yard, that is where they take robbers and put them behind bars, and look, in the middle, there is the clue and the code breaker." It read:

BITS AND PIECEs

It survived the great fire of 1666

And all of its bits

With no water just a writer and his daughter

And on your way the streets are full of news

And round the map are words and clues

1666/W.C.2/TEMPLE/NEWS/ BRIC-A-BRAC/WRITER

There was a tap on the door, Molly opened it and it was *The Shadow* having a kip. He was leaning up against the wall and his cane had fallen and knocked against the door.

Molly woke him up and he asked, "Have you got the map?" Molly replied, "Yes, and we have read it."

The Shadow said, "I know it is not Friday, but tomorrow I will be going to *The Shadow* convention in Leicester Square. There will be lots of Shadows everywhere; it's going to be a full moon with lots of people to scare. It is that time of year when I have most fun but I will be back with you on Saturday morning, so keep looking for the clues."

Saturday morning arrived and Mum said she was off shopping and that she would see them at five.

They grabbed their rucksacks and off they went with the old map in hand. Molly said, "The first clue must be The Temple." So they looked at their map, and, sure enough, there it was: The Temple on the Victoria Embankment.

As they walked they heard the nightingale sing all around Swan Lane and Angel Square. Matt said, "That sounds lovely."

Molly agreed and said, "It's a shame we had no seed." Off they went up Castle Raymond Street, over Blackfriars Bridge. The traffic had all come to a standstill and so they ran across to the other side of the street. Matt shouted, "Look, over there! another old ship." The sign said *H.M.S. President*. It was a warship painted in grey with guns pointing out from every angle, but there was nobody on board, just pigeons flying about. They had a good

look and then they turned round. Matt shouted,
"The **Temple**, over there."

They crossed the road and Molly said, "It's the start
of the codes," so she crossed off the first code.

Matt said to Molly, "I wonder what is in the
building." Just then, a little old lady passed by and
said, "That's where all the men with funny wigs sit
in court. They're Judges and Lawyers and keep the
law of the land. Is there anything else you would
like to know?"

"Yes, where can we read the news?" enquired Matt.

The little old lady looked up into the air and
suggested, "If you go up Arundel Street, walk to the
top and then you will find Fleet Street, it was where
all the newspapers were published, but no more,
only a plaque on the wall."

As she walked around the corner out of sight, her
shadow was left on the floor and they heard a click,
click, click of her walking stick. Was it *The Shadow*
in disguise or was it really a little old lady?

Matt and Molly followed her instructions and, at the
end of the street, just as she had said, there was
a plaque on the wall which had two codes, **News**
and **W.C.2.** Molly said, "That just leaves three
more to find."   Off they both went wondering where
they could be.   Matt and Molly walked and walked
until their feet nearly gave up. Then, across the

road they spotted *The Shadow* leaning up against the wall.

Matt and Molly walked across the road and told him they had nearly given up looking for the codes. He just gave a little giggle and floated away, and there, where he had been standing, was a plaque saying The Great Fire of London, this is where it all began in **1666**. Matt said, "That's another code, two more to go."

As they walked along, Molly remarked that what they must be looking for must be very old because, on the map, there were no new buildings and everywhere around were new office blocks. Then, in the distance, sticking out a mile was an old timber building with a sign saying 'The Old Curiosity Shop' immortalised by Charles Dickens. Matt said, "That must be one of the codes because he is a famous **wRITER** of Old London Town."

Matt and Molly walked across the road and looked in the window. They could see lots of old clocks, jewellery, pictures and a sign saying '**BRIC-A-BRAC**, please come and browse.' "That's the final code," said Matt. They went into the shop and the old doorbell rang. There was an oak counter with an old till on the top and there he was, *The Shadow*. He went, "Boo! What the dickens are you doing here?" Then he laughed and said, "Just one of my little jokes. Yes, you have broken the code. It was The Old Curiosity Shop. When you get home you will have to look around and your prize will be in the mirror."

All the way home Matt said to Molly, "How can it be in the mirror? A mirror is a mirror." They arrived back home, opened the front door and there, at the end of the hall, was the mirror. They dropped their bags and rushed to have a look, but it was only a mirror with a frame. Matt and Molly went into the lounge and again there was just a mirror in a frame, also the one in the snug was the same but still not a prize to be seen.

Matt and Molly went back into the hallway scratching their heads, hung their coats up on the stand and there, in the middle of the hat stand, was a little mirror in the shape of a heart.

Matt looked into the mirror and could see nothing but his face. Then, Molly stood back and took a look. She could see the wall behind her and a wooden candle-holder. She turned, looked round and, at the bottom of the candle, she found two gold rings with hearts in their centres. She gave one to Matt and they both slipped them on. All of a sudden, they felt a draught come through the letter box blowing all the way up the stairs. The Shadow was standing there and he said, "Keep your rings safe and they will bring you the love of your life. Good night."

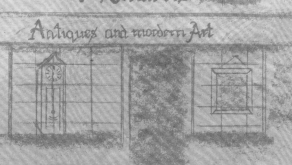

The
Old Curiosity Shop
immortalised by
Charles Dickens
Antiques and modern Art

CHAPTER 13

DIAMOND GEEZER

Matt and Molly did not see or hear The Shadow for a couple of days. He was out every night, probably giving some poor person a fright. Then, on Thursday evening, while they were sitting in front of the log fire in the lounge, he appeared and came and sat beside them.

Mum was busy baking in the kitchen and Dad was in the snug on his computer looking for investments. The Shadow just sat there and never said a word. Then Matt said, "Hello, mate, what have you been up to?"

The Shadow just yawned and told Matt he had been so tired and just needed a rest. It was so strange talking to a shadow with no face but they had got used to him and it was fun. Molly asked him, "Have you ever had a wife?"

The Shadow replied, "Yes, in another life."

Matt said, "Do you ever go on holiday?"

"I'm always on holiday, that is my life."

Molly enquired, "Why do you live here and not somewhere else?"

The Shadow sounded sad and replied, "My wife died here, in the study, and I promised I would never leave, so when I died my shadow was left and that is how it has always been."

Molly said, "We have never seen her, so where is she now?" **The Shadow** said, "I feel her everywhere but I have not seen her since 1863."

Matt asked him, "Has London changed much since then?"

The Shadow nodded his head, "Yes, the smog and the smoke has gone, so have the horses and carriages but now, with the buses and cars, there is a different kind of smog."

Molly asked him what was his favourite thing that he liked doing.

The Shadow said, "I follow people all day long. They think my shadow is them until they look in the shop window and then, in a flash, I slip away and find another person who likes to play. Just strangers I meet when I'm out in the street. I doff my hat and **tap** my cane. They rub their eyes but I'm gone so quickly."

Molly asked him, "Why is it that we cannot see your face?"

He replied, "I have no face for you to see, just a shadow that covers me. Now, I think I have said enough. Your Mum is calling you in for tea," and with that he floated upstairs to the window seat. He sat there, then drifted behind the curtains for a sleep.

After tea, Matt and Molly went upstairs to do their homework. As they walked past *The Shadow,* he bade them goodnight. Matt and Molly thought it was so lovely having their own shadow in the house to look after them.

The week went so quickly and school was hard work, especially maths and science. Finally, the last bell rang on Friday afternoon and the teacher said, "Have a good weekend and think of a good story that you can write about next week." Molly said to Matt, "We could have some fun and tell the teacher about Cotton House, and the other children will have to find out what it is about."

"A good idea," replied Matt.

On the way home they had some fun pretending they were shadows in the park. Eventually, they arrived home to find that Mum was doing some gardening at the front of the house. She looked at them and said, "You both seem very happy."

They said, "Yes, we have had a brilliant week."

When they got to their rooms, *The Shadow* had been

and left them both a note on their pillows. They were both similar but with different words.

Molly's note read, 'No. 13 is lucky for some and they are a girl's best friend.' And Matt's note read, 'You're a real diamond geezer and shine above the rest.'

They both walked out onto the landing and Matt said, "I wonder what that means. The diamonds sound amazing, but what's the geezer?"

That night after tea, Matt and Molly had a word with *The Shadow* and asked, "What's the geezer?"

He replied, "You will see: not far to go this time: out of the door and down the street this side of the river." When they got back upstairs, Matt opened the code breaker book and it was No. 13. Matt said, "Yes, lucky for some." And read the clues:

DIAMOND GEEZER

The badge above the door will tell you a lot more.
It's a place where kings and queens
Take their favourite things.
There are guards at the door
Dressed in clothes you don't see any more.
What's on show they cannot lend
As they are a girl's best friend

BEEF/CROWNS/BRIDGE/GHOSTS
QUEENS/DIAMONDS

The next morning they got up early and left home to break the code. Down to Tower Hill and there, in front of them, was the Royal Mint.

Molly said, "That's nothing to do with the code." Then, around the corner was the Dickens Inn, but that was not one of the codes either. They carried on walking round St. Catherine's Dock and all they found was a load of boats.

The Shadow was behind them and could see they were struggling, so he went up to Matt and tapped him on the shoulder and said, "Follow me." He floated up the steps and out of sight.

Matt and Molly ran up the steps and there, in front of them, was Tower Bridge. Hooters and horns sounded. They stood there in amazement as the roadway each side of the **bridge** started to move. Molly said, "That's the beginning of the third code breaker," and, as she said that, the road split in the middle and went up into the air like two big arms. Two tall ships sailed underneath, and then the bridge slowly came back down, allowing the traffic to cross once more.

As Matt and Molly walked along the side of the river, a group of tourists were talking and one said, "Look at the Beefeaters over there." Molly looked straight at Matt and said, "**Beef**, that's one of the first codes." "Perhaps it's to do with McDonalds?" Matt suggested. They walked round the corner and in front of them was a large stone-walled castle and there, above the gates, was a sign saying The Tower of London. At the side of the gate there was another sign on a post which read, 'Beware of the **ghosts** in the Tower.' They both shouted at the same time, "That's the fourth code!" Over in the corner were the Beefeaters. Matt and Molly walked up to the one guarding the gate and Matt said, "Hello, Mr. Beefeater." The Beefeater just smiled and asked them, "Have you come to see the **Crowns**, If so, I'll be glad to show you around?"

Matt nudged Molly and whispered, "The second code, cross it off." The Beefeater said, "The crowns belong to the owner of the house."

Matt asked, "Who might that be?"

"The **queen** of England," replied the Beefeater.

Molly crossed off the fifth code and the guard said, "That will be nine pounds each, please."

"How much?" gasped Molly. He looked so funny in his trousers and his funny coloured hat.

Just at that moment, *The Shadow* appeared. He stood next to the Beefeater and tapped him on the shoulder. As the man turned, all he could see was a shadow on the ground. Matt and Molly were shuffled in by the crowd and, before the guard could get back to his post, Matt and Molly were inside.

The place was full of people from far and wide, some from China and some from Holland.

In front of them was a man from Ireland. He was talking to himself saying, "I'd like to meet the **ghosts** of the Tower." With a grin Matt said, "That's number six, and that is the last." As they slowly walked along, they could see the crown jewels on display.

The crown looked beautiful with all the diamonds shining bright. A young man up ahead said, "You would have to be a real **diamond geezer** to wear these."

Molly said, "Marvellous, that's the code breaker done." They kept walking along and were fascinated by the history of the place; from the Duke of Wellington and his boots to the Beefeaters who guard the crown jewels and the Tower, where heads have been lost. Matt and Molly finished the tour and, at the exit gate, a Beefeater said, "Thank you for coming, especially your shadow!" As they looked around there was *The Shadow* sitting at a table in the Tower grounds. He told them he had got them a surprise and, as they sat down, burgers and fries were served before their eyes by another Beefeater.

After they had eaten lunch, they thanked the Beefeater for showing them the Tower.

He replied, "Just doing my duty."

When they arrived home, Mum said, "Hello, you're early. We are having burgers and fries for tea. Is that O.K.?"

Molly and Matt grinned at each other and replied, "That's just fine."

The next day was Sunday and was going to be a treat. Matt and Molly were going out for the day but Dad said it was a secret. That morning at breakfast, Dad told them they were going to a Castle for the day with a picnic.

They all got into the car and off they went. Over Westminster Bridge, along the Embankment, and to the outskirts of London.

Dad wondered whether the owners would be at home. Mum said, "She might be, but you won't know until we get there.

It was a lovely drive along the side of the River Thames and there, at the bottom of a long drive, was Windsor Castle. It stood so proudly at the end of the road. Dad parked the car and they had a long walk ahead.

When they were half way, Dad said, "Look, the flags are flying: it means they are at home." Matt said, "That's a lot of work. You'd think they would forget!" "No, they have many servants who take care of that," Dad replied. Mum whispered, "It's like looking after you three."

Dad bought four tickets and they all wandered in. The pictures on the wall were so big. There were knights in armour with swords and kings on horseback. At the end of the hallway there was a door upon which was written 'Library Private.'

Molly did not see the small sign. She opened the door and Mum, Dad and Matt followed her in. The room was amazing, with books on both sides and, at the end, was an old leather chair. To their surprise, a head popped up and said, "Hello, I'm the Queen. I believe you have come in the wrong door, this is private."

She looked at Matt and Molly and said, "I think I have seen you before, at the palace at the bottom of the Mall." Matt said, "I think so, but I'm not too sure."

They apologised for disturbing her, bowed their heads and left quietly. When they got outside the library, Dad asked "What was all that about? You never said you and Molly met the Queen."

Mum said, "Probably only in their dreams!"

They carried on looking around the castle and there were guards everywhere. Then, all of a sudden, one said, "Ssh, not a sound. Her Majesty is on her way round."

As the Queen walked past with corgis in tow she smiled at Matt and Molly and said, "I must take them for a walk before it gets dark, and before Philip comes in from the park."

They had such a lovely time in the castle and on the way out, they signed their names in the Visitors' Book and Matt wrote 'Thank you, Ma'am, we have had some fun.' Molly wrote, 'Your house needs cleaning. There's dust everywhere. I hope you don't mind me saying, but I've got it in my hair.'

On the way home Dad said, "Wow, that was fun. Shall we have a McDonalds?"

They all said, "No," so Pizza Hut was the place to go.

That night, they told *The Shadow* where they had been. "I know. I was there next to the Queen."

Matt said, "Oh yeah?"

The Shadow said, "Yes, I know. You went into the library and the Queen said she had seen you at Buckingham Palace." Molly looked at Matt and off they went to bed wondering if there was anywhere that *The Shadow* doesn't go.

He whispered in their ears, "No."

CHAPTER 14

STOP THE PLOT

That week, back at school, they had such fun writing about what they had done. Matt and Molly had all the children writing about Cotton House and the funfair and, yes, they both won the gold stars for the week.

In the middle of the week *The Shadow* told Matt and Molly that Saturday's code breaker was number fourteen in their book. So, on Friday night after school, they read the clue:

STOP THE PLOT

It is 1605 right in front of your very eyes.
He stopped the fuse,
Now you're confused,
With no big bang.
The bell still rang
And the people of old London town
Jumped up and down
Throwing him half crowns
To The Shadow on the ground.

MINSTER / W.C. 1 / PLOT / NO BANG / WEST

On Friday night, after school, they read the clue and the code breaker over and over again but not a thought came to mind.

The next morning they were on the trail. Down the Embankment towards W.C.1., which they knew would be on a sign at Charing Cross. When they got there **The Shadow** said, "Another clue which might be on the way is: It's a cube. What do you say?"

Matt and Molly turned and looked around. Over on the other side of the river was a tall building all lit up and on the roof a sign said 'OXO.' Molly said, "That's the clue." So they turned around and went back across Blackfriars Bridge. When they reached the other side Molly said, "This is not W.C.1." Matt agreed, "Yes, you are right."She said, "Now, no more mistakes."

Matt replied, "Wait a minute! It was not me it was **The Shadow** teasing us."

The Shadow appeared laughing and said, "Sorry about that, my little joke, just keeping you on your toes." Matt shouted, "It wasn't funny you know!" As they walked along Molly commented, "Now that's a sight to see." It was a big yellow duck floating up the river but not a real one, just a car or truck. It had many tourists on board and a sign which read, 'The London Duck Tours.'

All of a sudden, the truck came out of the water and drove off down the road, showing everybody the city sights of old London town. When it returned, it drove straight back into the water and carried on down the river to see the rest of the Thames.

As they walked along, they came to Savoy Street.

Matt suggested they walk up there. When they reached the end of the road, there, in front of them, was the Savoy Hotel. The front door was going round and round. Molly stepped in and was whizzed through the door and fell to the ground, Matt followed and the doorman said, "May I help you?"

She replied, "I think I have hurt my leg, but I am sure I will be alright."

The doorman enquired, "I have not seen you before. Are you staying here in the Hotel?" Matt nodded his head and said, "Yes, that's right." The doorman suggested a cold drink and a cake to settle them down. "Yes, please," they both replied and the doorman showed them to the lounge.

It was beautiful with tall ceilings and windows. Molly thought the waiters were dressed like penguins. In the middle of the room was an old white piano, and as their drinks were brought to the table a man came and sat at the piano and started playing. After he had finished everybody applauded.

Just then, the waiter brought over a cakestand full of pastries. There were muffins, jam tarts and all sorts of cream cakes. The man in the penguin suit said, "May I have your room number, young man?"

Matt joked and said, "Number forty-four." "Thank you," said the penguin, "Two cokes and eight pastries, see you later at dinner."

Matt said, "Yes, please."

Molly grabbed Matt and said, "Quickly, let's get out of here." They walked to the doorway and the doorman said, "Hello, off out again?" "Yes," Matt replied, "We have left our hats and brollies in the Strand."

As they walked off Molly complained that her stomach was so full but only because she ate most of the cakes. Matt said, "Look over the road at the sign. It says **W.C.7.** That's one of the codes, so what is next?"

Molly replied, "Plot, perhaps a plot of land." "I don't know," answered Matt, "And what does bang mean?"

At that moment, an old van went past and it backfired. The noise echoed across the bridge and there, at the end, was a sign: Westminster Bridge. "That's two of the codes **minster** and **west**!" As Matt and Molly crossed the road, in front of them was Big Ben, a tall tower with a beautiful old clock.

As the hands moved to midday the bells rang. There was an old man with his grandson next to them and he said, "It's a beautiful clock. What is its name?" The little boy replied, "Big Ben, of course." The old man looked at him and shook his head, "No, the name Big Ben is not the clock. It is the name of the bell that rings."

Matt said to Molly, "I didn't know that, did you?" They carried on walking and then, around the corner, were the Houses of Parliament, but no plot. Over on a wall, people were looking at a copper plaque. It was shining brightly in the sun and it read:

This plaque is here just to say

That on the date of 1605

A man and his friends walked into

Parliament with barrels of gun powder

And a big fuse wire was laid

But the day was saved by

The Shadow of Old London Town

Matt said, "Wow, what about that, *The Shadow* never told us he had done that."Molly replied, "I don't believe it. I think it is all made up." Then there was a **tap tap tap** and a pat on their backs and Matt and Molly went spinning around until, completely dizzy, they fell to the ground.

When they stood up, it was dark and very foggy and the air was full of smoke from old coal fires. "What's happened?" said Matt.

The Shadow said, "I have taken you back in time," Then from out of the mist, an old horse and cart appeared. There were lots of men in jackets and breeches with hoods over their heads. The cart was taken around the side of the Houses of Parliament and then the men started unloading old barrels from the cart.

Matt and Molly were hiding round the corner and they heard one of the men shouting, "Watch out, you will blow us all up." Another man said, "O.K., Guy Fawkes." They carried all the barrels into the building and the horse and cart went off down the road. As some of the men walked past, Matt and Molly heard them say they would be back later to blow up the Houses of Parliament.

Matt and Molly sat there in the fog talking to each other, "How can we stop them? This must be the **plot** and another code."

As they walked round the side of the building, there was the fuse wire ready to be lit. They heard a noise out in the street, and then a guard walked towards them with an old lady next to him. He said to her, "You've lost the plot, so on your way home."

Matt said, "Hello, I think you should know we can stop the plot."

The guard said, "What are you talking about?"

Matt and Molly showed him the fuse wire and told him that they heard the men say that they would be back later.

The guard said, "Are you sure?" Matt replied, "Without a shadow of doubt."

The guard ran to get more help and when he returned he told Matt and Molly to wait in the woods in case there was a big bang. Molly said, "That is the last code."

Everybody hid in the woods out of sight, waiting for Guy Fawkes to arrive, but he came in from the other way and they did not see him. He lit the fuse wire, then, out of the fog, floated The Shadow and a gust of wind put the fuse wire out. Guy Fawkes shouted out and suddenly the policemen grabbed him and his men and took them down to the police station.

Matt and Molly were thanked for their good deed and the King arrived in his carriage and announced, "Thank you for saving Parliament House and here is a little present." There were two velvet pouches but not to be opened until they got home. As they walked out of the police station they walked back into their own time with taxis and buses and their own shadow.

Matt said, "We have helped save the Houses of Parliament and stopped the plot, there was no big bang but another code broken and another prize."

When they arrived home they opened the velvet pouches and inside each bag was a small gold bell of Big Ben.

Molly said, "What an amazing day."

That night The Shadow said, "Thank you for helping today. You must look after your bells and they will remind you of November 5th and why it is called Firework night."

As Matt and Molly looked out of the window, the London sky was full of colour with fireworks bursting everywhere. They could hear Big Ben ringing in the distance and they had many a laugh telling people about Big Ben being the bell and not the clock.

CHAPTER 15

DON'T TAKE THE BISCUIT

The next morning Molly woke Matt up and asked him, "Did we really help stop the plot?" Matt replied, "It does ring a bell!"

At breakfast Mum and Dad announced that they were going out to dinner on Saturday night to a very special restaurant. Mum said, "We have arranged a baby-sitter. We know you are not babies any longer but it will be a long evening, and I'm sure you will like her."

Saturday morning arrived and when they woke up there was a note under Molly's door. It read, 'Tonight is the night for the next code breaker, so look in the old leather book and go to code fifteen.' The book was getting thinner and thinner as they were breaking the codes, but the new book they were writing was getting longer with lots of illustrations of Old London Town.

Matt told Molly that he was nearly up to date with the pictures to the next chapter, and perhaps she could slow down with the story and give him a little more time to finish the drawings.

The note read, 'This code is not very easy to crack so don't take the biscuit and get in a flap.'

DON'T TAKE THE BISCUIT

It's somewhere classy to eat

And it's not out in the street.

Remember to be suited and booted.

All the glasses will be fluted

It's top biscuit

So don't forget to eat it.

STARS/CHEESE/SUITS/PIANO/ BISCUIT/BUBBLES

Matt said to Molly, "But we can't go as Mum and Dad said they are going out for dinner tonight." *The Shadow* heard them and said, "That's O.K., we will sort something out. Now, look at the book and try and work it out."

All day long they kept thinking about how they could crack the code breaker without going out. While Mum and Dad were upstairs getting ready, Matt and Molly came out of the lounge and saw that the hat and cane had gone. At that moment the phone rang, Matt picked it up and it was Mum and Dad's friends who said they were not well and would have to postpone the dinner date.

Mum asked Matt and Molly if they would like to come to the restaurant. They both replied, "Yes, please." As they ran upstairs to change Mum shouted, "Best clothes, please!"

On the way back down Molly asked Matt, "What are we going to do about the code?"

The Shadow was standing at the bottom of the stairs and said, "I have heard about the change of plan, but, to be honest, it won't change a thing just carry on and play the code breaker as normal."

Mum shouted out, "The taxi has arrived but I still haven't been able to contact the baby-sitter. I will have to leave a message on the door."

Everybody jumped into the taxi and the driver asked, "Where to, mate?"

Dad said, "To the best restaurant in town," and whispered to him through the glass, and off he drove.

Mum said, "You will both love this place, there will be lots of stars." Matt took the code book out of his pocket and there it was: the first code STARS. Before they knew it the taxi driver said, "I will drop you off here because of the traffic jam, it's two minutes round the corner." Just as he said that, there, in front of them, was a tall elegant building all lit up like a Christmas tree and a sign saying The Ritz.

Dad said, "It's really a big **CHEESe BISCUIT**," and laughed.

"Yes," said Molly, another two codes. The doorman opened the door and said, "Good evening, sir. Do you have a reservation?"

"Yes, we have a table booked for 8.00p.m."
"Certainly, sir, please come this way and I will show you to your table."

The waiter asked them all what they would like to drink and Mum said, "I would like some **BUBBLES**."

Matt asked, "What do you mean?"

Mum replied, "Champagne, of course."

The waiters were all dressed in beautiful **SUITS**, and Molly whispered in Matt's ear, "Another code and only one to go. It's a bit spooky. It's as if Mum and Dad are playing the game as well."

As the waiter brought their drinks to the table a man in a white suit with a bow tie walked past them and sat at the **PIANO**. Matt nudged Molly and said, "That's the last one. It is the easiest code breaker we have ever had to do." As the pianist played, to their amazement they saw *The Shadow* standing next to him and he suddenly started to dance to the tune of *'Singing in the rain.'*

The pianist thought he was brilliant. Matt said to Molly, "I didn't know he was that light on his feet!"

Mum frowned and said, "Look, he is wearing the same hat and cane that hangs in our hall."

Molly said, "It can't be, the man is too tall!" *The Shadow* finished his dance routine and as he bowed and started to walk away everybody applauded and the pianist said to him, "Bertie, the same time next week?"

He nodded his head and whispered, "Without a shadow of doubt."

The food was delicious and the music was fun.

After dinner Dad settled the bill and Mum suggested they go for a walk. Their walk took them all the way down The Mall and back again, singing and dancing the same song *The Shadow* had danced to.

Eventually, they got back to Trafalgar Square where Dad flagged down a taxi to take them home. As they jumped in the driver said, "Hello, didn't I pick you up earlier?"

"Yes, so you know where we are going."

When they arrived back home there was a note on the door. It was from the baby-sitter. It said, 'Sorry I was late, but I had a problem with me and my shadow!'

When they got back indoors the hat and cane were gone.

Mum muttered, "Now I know there's something strange going on." She went into the kitchen to put the kettle on and when she came back into the hall, there they were; the hat and cane were back again. **The Shadow** was obviously playing games with Mum.

The Shadow popped upstairs to see Matt and Molly before they went to sleep and said, "I heard you say that this code breaker was too easy, so next time I will make it harder, but until then just think of children you will meet." As he floated back through the door Matt said, "I think it is about children at school, I think it is going to be just as easy."

Just then **The Shadow** stuck his head round the door and said, "Before you ask: your treat tonight was the cheese biscuit, The Ritz, ha, ha, ha."

CHAPTER 16

CHILDREN YOU WILL MEET

The next week at school Matt and Molly and their classmates were asked to draw a picture of one of London's most prominent buildings. Matt drew Tower Bridge with a shadow cast over it and Molly drew Buckingham Palace, also with a shadow over the building. The teacher thought that it was funny that they had both drawn their pictures in the same way. She asked them, "Is there a point to this, or have I missed the plot?"

Matt said, "Guy Fawkes, he had a plot," and Molly replied, "He also had a shadow."

The teacher remarked, "O.K., the shadow can stay."

As she walked away there was a tap, tap, tap. It was the teacher's shoes; they sounded just like the cane *The Shadow* carried.

Night after night they completed their homework, and then, on Thursday evening, after they had eaten their supper, *The Shadow* asked them, "Would you like to hear a story about my friends, the Pearly Kings and Queens?"

Matt and Molly replied, "Yes, please."

So Matt put a note on his door and it read, 'Quiet, please! Homework in progress,' and Molly did the same.

Matt and Molly followed *The Shadow* up to the attic. He opened the window and then said, "Now, shut your eyes and I will take you on a journey." They closed their eyes and dreamt that they were flying up in the sky and, as they looked down on Old London Town, Nelson's Column appeared. They flew round twice and Matt touched Nelson's nose. As they flew off, Nelson sneezed and blew them all the way to Chelsea.

As they floated down to the ground, *The Shadow*

said, "Now, bow your heads," and as they did a voice shouted, "Hello, my darlings!" It was an old lady who was wearing a brightly-coloured suit covered in sequins and buttons. "Hello, Bertie," she said and enquired, "How have you been?"

The Shadow nodded his head and said, "Just fine, and how about you?"

"Well, we have been to see the Queen today and so we are all tired and worn out."

Then, from out of a gateway walked her family: her sons, daughters, uncles and aunties. They were all dressed alike, in sequins and buttons. The old lady said, "Put a pound in the hat and we will all dance around. All the money goes to the children's home."

It was lovely to see the Pearly Kings and Queens. Molly and Matt said their goodbyes and that they hoped to see them again.

All of a sudden, *The Shadow* went **tap tap tap** and as they opened their eyes they found themselves back in the attic and Molly said, "Wow, that was so real." Then they heard Mum shout up the stairs, "It's time for bed." Matt and Molly went off to sleep dreaming of the Pearly Kings and Queens.

The following morning there was a knock at their doors. It was Mum. She said, "Come on, you two, not another lie in. Up you get and off to school."

When they arrived at school the teacher said, "Today we are going to talk about kings and queens of England's past." The children all sat and listened to a story she read and after she had finished, she asked the children to draw their favourite King and Queen.

At the end of the day the teacher collected all their drawings. Matt and Molly had both drawn the same, Pearly Kings and Queens. The teacher asked them, "How do you know about the Pearly Kings and Queens?"

Matt replied, "We have met them. They are our friends. We could ask them to come to the school, they will need paying, but all the money donated goes to the children's home."

The teacher said, "Perhaps you could ask them."

That evening, Matt and Molly asked *The Shadow* if he could help. He said, "Yes, I will have a word with my friends, the Pearly Kings and Queens." So off he went and when he returned he told Matt and Molly that they would love to come to the school at the end of the week.

The school hall was full and, as the Pearly Kings and Queens arrived, all the children stood up and cheered. First, there was a speech about their history and then their life today in old London town.

Then they danced and did their party piece. All the children put money in their hats and, after school, the Pearly Kings and Queens donated the money they had collected that afternoon to the children's hospital at Great Ormond Street.

The teacher was so pleased and said to the class, "How brilliant was that?" The children did nothing else for days but talk about the Pearly Kings and Queens.

Friday night had arrived and Half term was just about to begin, it was the last holiday before Christmas. Matt and Molly had stacks of homework that would keep them busy and Mum and Dad had very hectic weeks, but to make up for it they had booked a lovely winter skiing holiday for the four of them, which they knew the twins would love.

That night Matt looked at the code breaker book. There was a note inside and it read:

CHILDREN YOU WILL MEET

This place is a real treat.

Lots of children you will meet.

The shop is very old

So wrap up and don't get cold.

It sounds like apples

But it is not a chapel.

It's in W.C.2

So hopefully for you

It's not Scrabble

HAM/FUN/REGENT/W.C.2./CIRCUS

In the morning Matt and Molly looked at the map of Old London Town looking for the code REGENT. They searched and searched but there was nothing to be found. Molly said, "What about the Ham? Perhaps it is an old butcher's shop." They scratched their heads at the word circus. So, they packed a bag with food and drink and walked out of the front door. When they got to the bottom of the steps, Mum shouted out of the window above, "Don't be late home as Dad and I are going out tonight to Piccadilly Circus, and we hope the sitter turns up this time."

Molly and Matt said, "We're not going far." As they walked, Matt looked at the map and there in the middle was Piccadilly Circus, so they decided that was the place to go.

On the way they came to Charing Cross and, over the road, was Scotland Yard with a big chrome sign shining bright. As they walked past, two policemen were coming towards them, Matt said, "Hello, hello." The policemen said, "Are you taking the Mickey?"

"No, just being polite," Matt said. "By the way, the sign says Scotland Yard. Is it out the back?"

The policeman said, "No, there is no yard just the jail, so, be on your way or you might have to stay."

"No, thank you," said Matt and off they went.

Matt and Molly walked past the Mall and as they looked up, the flag was flying. Molly said, "She must be at home."

As they turned the corner there was an old lady who was dressed as a mime. She stood very still and only moved when people put money in her hat and then she would go "Boo!"

Matt asked her, "Are you from the circus?"and in a deep voice she groaned, "No, so on your way."

Molly cried out, "Everybody is moving us on today, do we smell?"

Eventually, Matt and Molly arrived at Piccadilly Circus and there, in the middle of the road, was another policeman controlling the traffic. As he walked back towards them Matt asked, "Excuse me, where is the Circus?"

He replied, "There is not one here, just a lot of traffic and people in a rush."

Matt said, "Never mind, at least we have found the code **CIRCUS** and **W.C.2.**"

The twins kept finding the codes; one after another. Regent Street was next. Molly cried "Code, code it is written in the sign **REGENT**."

Across the road was the big department store John Lewis. Matt said, "Look, we will go in there and ask Mr. Lewis where the circus is, he will know!" They walked through the doors and saw a lady at one of the tills. They asked to see Mr. Lewis, but she laughed and said, "No, it is his day off but can I help?"

Matt asked, "Where is the circus around here?"

She answered, "No, Oxford Circus is just a name but I'm sure a hundred years ago or more there would have been one, hence the names."

Matt and Molly thanked her and off they went. Outside the shop was a wooden bench and they sat down for a bite to eat. While they were there one mum with a pushchair walked past. The toddler was crying and mum said, "You will have to wait until we get to Hamleys, then I will buy you a little toy and you can have some fun." Molly grinned and told Matt, "Those are the other two codes, **HAM** of Hamleys and **FUN**."

So, off they went and followed the pushchair and the screams, and there, across the road, was Hamleys, the finest toy shop in the world. As they walked through the doors the screams stopped as every little child was bewitched by the magic of the toy shop.

Matt and Molly had a whale of a time playing with the toys and reading books, then, suddenly, an old man with a white beard appeared from nowhere and said to them, "How do you like my shop?" Molly replied, "It's lovely."The old man told them he had been there for seventy years. "Surely not," Matt exclaimed. "Yes," he said, "When toys were all made from wood."

The old man pointed to the corner of the toy shop. There were two old wooden doors. Molly and Matt followed him and he asked them, "What does it say above the door?" Molly looked at the sign and said, "It's all in a muddle." The old man replied, "It is a code and if you take all the capital letters what does it spell?"

Matt shouted out, *"The Shadow* of the past!"

The old man replied, "Yes, you're right. Would you like to go through the doors and see what is on the other side?" "Yes," they both replied.

The old man took a large old key from out of his pocket and put it into the lock, he turned the key and the doors slowly opened. They walked through and the doors slammed tight behind them. Matt and Molly cried, "Wow!" They were in a room and from the floor to the ceiling were ropes with toys hanging from them. It was like an old circus from the past with wooden carts and wooden rides. There were books all made from leather and a sign advertising the new author of the day, Beatrix Potter.

Matt said to Molly, "Her books are still being published today; I can remember when Mum and Dad bought us a copy."

The old man said, "You have gone back in time once again and what do you think of the wonderful toys?" They both replied, "We think they are better than some of the rubbish toys today!"

The old man said, "I'm glad you said that. It has made my day."

There were marbles of all shapes and sizes and puppets on strings and clowns hanging from the ropes. Then the old man said, "Now, take a seat, as the show is about to start."

Matt and Molly looked around and, apart from them and their shadow on the ground, nobody else was there, just the old man.

In front of them was an old theatrical box with curtains draped across the front. Suddenly, the curtains flew open and two puppets popped their heads up and one said, "Hello kids, my name is Punch and this is Judy." They were so funny. They kept beating each other with sticks and sausages, while Punch cried "That's the way to do it!" Finally, Mr. Policeman popped his head up and took them all away.

The old white bearded man said, "The show is finished and I hope you enjoyed seeing what made the children of the past laugh, play and have fun."

As Matt and Molly went out of the old wooden doors to the toy shop they heard the key turn in the lock and, as they turned, the key dropped to the floor. Molly picked up the key and went to put it back in the lock, but, to their amazement, the doors and the old man had disappeared. They looked at each other and thought, how could that be? Then a man in a suit said, "I think that is my key." As he walked away he, too, disappeared leaving just his shadow on the floor.

All of a sudden there was a tap tap tap and there stood *The Shadow*. He whispered, "That was fun but really it was just for me."

On the way home Matt and Molly played Hop Scotch easily beating *The Shadow,* who could not count.

When they arrived home Mum said that she and Dad were going out that night to Piccadilly as Dad had a business dinner to attend. George, Mum's literary agent, and his wife Dorothy, whom the twins knew, were going to come and sit for a couple of hours.

Matt and Molly ate their tea and were sitting in the lounge next to the roaring fire, writing and drawing the new chapter to their book, when the doorbell rang. Mum answered the door and said good evening to her friends and took them through to Matt and Molly, whom they had not seen since they were little and living in Hong Kong.

Mum said to George, "I must say, you do suit your new white beard. It's quite strange seeing you with one." Dad walked into the lounge and said, "Sorry, we're running a little late. We must go."

George and Dorothy sat down with Matt and Molly. George said, "I have brought a little book that was one of your Mum's first to be published, twenty years ago when she started writing. Would you like me to read it to you?"

Matt and Molly said, "Yes, please." So George said, "I will begin."

There was once a little orphan girl who lived in an old convent on Angel Hill and was taught by the nuns.

Every day, after her lessons had finished, she saw the nuns carrying spades and forks and empty baskets down the hall and out through the oak doors. One day, the little girl noticed the door had been left open, she thought to herself, 'Shall I?' and then thought 'No,' the rule was no children were allowed to go outside without permission.

Every day the nuns would bring back baskets full of vegetables, fruits, bread and cakes. But, one day, the little girl decided to go round the building to the other side. She followed the old stone wall but ended up back where she had started at the main doors. There was no garden, no trees and no bees, so how could the nuns fill their baskets with fruit and vegetables without a garden, and why did they need the spades and forks?

One afternoon, after class, she could not bear it any longer, she had to find out where the nuns went to fill their baskets. So, as Sister Angel was the last one out of the door, she followed them into the courtyard and there they all got their spades and forks and flew up into the air.

The little girl grabbed a spare fork and up she flew over the wall, up into the sky and landed on a cloud. There, she could see the nuns picking fruits of all kinds just lying in the clouds. She picked up an apple and took a bite but it just evaporated into juice. One of the nuns saw her and said, "No, you can't eat it until you're back at the convent. Up here they are just like water but, after we have blessed them on the way down they turn into solid fruit and vegetables."

Sister Mary said, "By the way, you should not be up here."

The little girl replied, "Sorry, sister, but I was just curious." Then one of the nuns asked, "Baskets all filled?" and down they all flew through the clouds.

When they got back to the convent the little girl asked, "We have no bread and cakes have you forgotten them?" Just at that moment the baker arrived. The sister asked the little girl, "Do you think we grow them as well?"

Everybody sat down for dinner and prayers were said, "To all of us at Angel Hill may we be blessed forever more and may the clouds give us our daily bread and vegetables and especially our spades and forks!"

George said, "Well, I bet Mum doesn't remember this one, a little young for you but I thought you would both like to hear her first attempt at writing."

"I believe you have some homework?"

Matt and Molly said good night and they went to their rooms.

The next morning Mum said, "I hear George and Dorothy read you one of the first books that I wrote twenty years ago, it's good to know that after all this time people are still reading them. What are you up to today?"

Matt and Molly replied, "We would love to go and see the nuns and the convent at Angel Hill."

Molly asked, "Is it far from here?"

Mum said, "I don't think the convent is there any more. I think it is just big office blocks but, wait a minute, I think I remember being told there is a garden and the old bell still remains. If you do go you must listen out for the bell. You must walk along the Embankment and opposite Swan Lane Pier is Angel Pass which is where the convent used to be, and before that it was a monastry."

Matt and Molly set off and followed Mum's directions. She was right; there were many offices towering up into the sky. Then, as they walked between two office blocks there was a small park and there, under a cherry tree, was a park bench.

The twins sat down but could not see the bell, and then, suddenly at eleven thirty, a bell started to ring over in the corner of the stone walled garden.

Matt and Molly ran over to have a look and, sure enough, there was the bell being rung by an old lady dressed in a nun's habit. "Hello," she said.

Matt replied, "Our Mum told us about the bell and she wrote a book about Angel Hill and the old convent."

The nun asked their mother's name and she replied, "I remember her well. We taught her to read and write in 1969, but after she left us there was a fire and the convent was never rebuilt. The bell is the only thing that remains."

The nun took an old leather book from out of her bag, opened the book and said, "Look, here is your mother's name, and it says 'top marks in her class.' I remember her writing the book. Perhaps you would like to ring the bell at mid-day?"

Matt and Molly replied, "Yes, we would love to." They sat there looking at their watches and then, from far away, they heard Big Ben strike twelve. On the count of three they rang the bell twelve times.

As they turned around the nun was gone, all there was left on the floor was her bag. Molly opened it up and inside was a note. It read 'Please find in this bag a beautiful cream bible. Keep it with you wherever you go and it will always remind you of the convent and the old bell tucked away in the corner of Old London Town. Please give my regards to your mum. God bless," and she had signed it Sister Angel.

Matt and Molly walked back home with thoughts of the old convent that was no longer there, with only tall buildings looking down on a small park with a bench under a cherry tree.

"Does anyone know why the bench is there?" "No, I don't think so, just somewhere to sit."

When they arrived home, Mum asked, "How did it go?"

Matt and Molly were so excited. They said, "We found the old bell and we met Sister Angel who taught you at school."Mum replied, "I remember her, but I thought she had passed away. Are you sure?"

"Yes," they both replied.

Molly said, "She remembered you and how you loved writing and the book you wrote about them and life in the convent."

Matt said, "Sister Angel let us ring the bell at mid-day and then she disappeared, but she left us this beautiful bible with a note. "Look!"

Mum read the note Sister Angel had left them and said, "You must treasure this as it has been left to you from a very special lady. Now, how about you go upstairs and get washed and changed. Then we can watch a film before tea."

As Matt and Molly walked up the stairs, there on the landing was *The Shadow*. Matt told him that they had rung an old bell that had belonged to the old convent. *The Shadow* said, "Yes, and angels fly."

Molly replied, "Yes, they do actually. Good night to you, Bertie."

CHAPTER 17

THE PLACE TO SHOP IN TOWN

It was a bright but cold winter's morning. Matt and Molly were still fast asleep. *The Shadow* looked in both their rooms and said, "This is not a good start to the day." He went and opened their curtains and shouted to them both, "Come on, get up my friends! We have a game to play." Matt and Molly got washed and dressed and went down for their breakfast. Thanking *The Shadow* on the way down, they whispered, "We owe you one Bertie, a shock, that is!"

After they had eaten breakfast, they went and sat in the snug. Molly opened the code breaker book and there was a note. It read, 'Only two codes to go, you choose which one is next. It is either; Numbers will take you to this door or The place to shop in town."

Matt asked, "Which one, Molly?"

Molly replied, "Shall we leave the numbers to last as it sounds like Maths to me?" They both agreed.

All week they played games with the children next door; finally, Friday night arrived.

The Shadow was outside following an old man

pretending to hold his hand, the old man turned around and Bertie simply fell to the ground; just then, Matt opened the window and shouted out, "What is the next code?"

The Shadow shouted back, "Can't you see that I am busy playing a game?"

That night, *The Shadow* slipped a note under Molly's door, it read, 'I know you have made your minds up already so we will leave the numbers to the end.'

That night they thought of the shops they had seen but this one must be the best. Molly went to Matt's room and said, "I will read you the clue and the code."

THE PLACE TO SHOP IN TOWN

It's the place to be seen

And it's all green.

The owner is Mr. A.

He's the one to pay

Knights and bridge will take you here

But don't forget it will be dear

MR. A/DIAMOND/S/GREEN/TOYS/ FOOD HALL

The next morning at breakfast Matt said to Molly, "It's got to be a shop of some kind." Mum walked into the room and said, "Please can you get me some groceries from the market?"

Matt and Molly wrapped up warm and off they went. It was a beautiful morning with the sun shining through the clouds. They walked across the road and up towards Petticoat Lane.

The market was huge and seemed to go on forever. The man on the first stall shouted, "Try one of my apples! It is my treat." By the time they got to the end of the street their stomachs were full and not a penny spent, but they still had not bought any of the items on Mum's list. Matt suggested to Molly, "If we play the code breaker perhaps we can buy the groceries at the Food Hall?" Molly thought that was a good idea and off they went.

As usual, they walked for a while then decided to jump on a bus. The bus conductor said, "Where is it to be?" Matt replied, "To the best shop to be seen in and we think it is green!"

The bus conductor said, "I know where you mean and it's definitely **GREEN**, and that will be two pounds please." Molly said to Matt, "That is the first code."

The bus conductor said to them, "It is owned by **M.** **A.**" Matt said, "Yes, the second code."

The bus drove off down the road and Matt and Molly had no idea where they were going.

After a while, the conductor came back upstairs and said to Matt and Molly, "The Christmas lights are all up in Oxford Street and that will be a treat." He asked them if they were on a day out. They replied, "No, we're just out buying Mum's groceries." He told them where they we're going was expensive and they would be better off with the market, and they told him that they wanted to go to the best shop in town.

A lady came upstairs, sat opposite them and put her bags down on the seat. One large green bag fell to the floor. Molly helped and picked the bag up for her, and, on the side, it said Harrods. The lady thanked her and the bus came to a halt, and there, in front of them, was the place to be seen, Harrods, all in GREEN.

The bus conductor said, "You have got one hour and then I will be back on the opposite side of the street if you would like a free ride home."

Matt said, "Yes, please."

Matt and Molly jumped off the bus, the shop was massive and through the front doors they walked. They looked around but could not see any groceries, so, they went up the stairs and ended up on the top floor.

A lady walking by said to her husband, "We must go to the ground floor to the FOOD HALL."

Matt said, "The third code." so they quickly followed the couple down the stairs.

On the next floor the sign said TOYS. Molly said, "That's one of the codes, let's go and have a look."

Matt replied, "What about the groceries?"

"Yes, you're right, of course, but let's go and have a look at the toys first!"

The toy department was huge and they had a good look around. Just as they turned to walk out, they noticed their Mum's name, J. Jennings, best seller, and when they took a closer look, there, on the shelf, were all of the books that she had ever written, including the first one, *Angel Hill* which George had read to them the other evening.

Molly said, "This is definitely the best shop in town."

So, Matt and Molly carried on down the staircase to the next floor. There they saw a sign that said DIAMONDS. "Another code," said Matt.

Eventually they arrived at the Food Hall where they managed to get the goodies on Mum's shopping list. As they queued up at the till, Molly said to Matt, "Do you know, we have not had the pleasure of seeing *The Shadow* today. I wonder where he is."

At last it was Matt and Molly's turn to be served.

The lady started to count, "Five, six, seven, eight, twelve pounds, please."

Molly took the money out of her pocket but she only had ten pounds. They had spent two pounds on the bus trip. They were holding everybody up.

Molly said, "We have not got enough money, I'm very sorry you will have to take a couple of items off as we only have ten pounds." So the lady rang the bell.

An older gentleman came over to the till and said, "What is the problem?"

The lady replied, "They are two pounds short."

The man looked at them and said, "Is your Mum the children's book authoress J. Jennings? I heard you talking upstairs just now about your Mum and her books. She is our top selling authoress," and he told the lady on the till to waive the bill and give them one of their special green bags for their groceries.

Matt and Molly thanked him and he saw them to the main door, and said to them, "Give my regards to your Mum; I can't wait for her new book to arrive."

Matt replied, "Who shall I say?"

"Just tell her it was **Mr.** **A.**, and, by the way, give my regards to Bertie, *The Shadow.*"

Molly asked, "How do you know Bertie?"

Mr. A. replied, "He's always on the third floor reading your Mum's books. It seems the only way to get him out is at closing time when all the lights go out."

Molly and Matt said, "Thank you for everything Mr. A. And, as Arnold Schwarzenegger says, "We'll be back!"

The twins crossed the road and stood waiting for their free bus ride, knowing that they had cracked the entire code breaker.

The bus arrived and on they jumped, followed by The Shadow as the bus drove away. He was hanging onto the pole all the way to the next stop, and then he decided to get off.

As the bus turned into Oxford Street, Matt shouted, "Wow, look Molly, the Christmas lights - they seem to go on forever." They were excited that Christmas was so near. Finally, they walked back through the door at Nightingale Square. Mum walked into the hallway and said, "Where have you been? I have been waiting for the groceries."

Matt replied, "We have bought the best you can buy in town."

Mum giggled, "I can see that by the bag, and I bet there is no change?"

Matt said, "Yes, you have got change because Mr. A. who owns the shop let us have them free."

"You saw Mr. A.?"

"Yes, he said your books sell more than any others in the store and he cannot wait for your new book." Molly said, "Oh, and by the way, he said 'Hello."

Mum thanked Matt and Molly for going all that way and said, "Now, please go out to play and I will call you when tea is ready."

When they got outside Matt said to Molly, "Do you realise we have only got one code breaker to go? It is quite sad."

After tea, Matt and Molly were playing Scrabble again and they heard their parents talking in the kitchen. Dad told Mum, "We're off again. I have been promoted. New York, here we come! At least we will have Christmas here with the kids, but New Year will be in New York."

Mum replied, "How are we going to tell Matt and Molly? They have settled in so well and have been having so much fun, but, yes, I know it has to be done."

That night Matt and Molly could not sleep and lay in their beds thinking of all the friends they had made and games they had played.

The Shadow popped into Molly's room and asked, "What is the matter? You seem upset?"

"Yes," she replied, "we're moving again and there is nothing we can do."

Matt heard them talking and came into Molly's room and sat by Bertie.

The Shadow said to Molly and Matt, life is like a train on a track, sometimes it keeps rolling and sometimes it stops, and when it does you have to take a step back and learn as much as you can. You have been here nearly a year and it is now time to get back on that track. It is not your Dad's fault. It is the bank, and one day you will understand when you're married, working and with children of your own."

Molly and Matt thanked him for being so kind and for being a very good friend.

Before *The Shadow* left, he said, "Come on, you two. Cheer up and let's make this the best Christmas for you to remember. I have been told that your birthday is on Christmas Eve and before then we must crack the last code."

Matt and Molly agreed, "Yes you're right. Good night, Bertie."

CHAPTER 18

NUMBERS WILL TAKE YOU TO THIS DOOR

The next morning at breakfast, Dad and Mum told Matt and Molly about the move.

Molly just sat there with tears in her eyes and

Matt said, "Do you know what? Life is like being on a train, sometimes chugging along and sometimes stopping. When it stops you get off and learn about life, and then jump back on again."

Dad replied, "Yes, you're so right."

Matt and Molly went off to school. Mum wiped a tear from her eye and said, "That wasn't so bad after all."

December was very busy at the school for Matt and Molly, with the end of year exams and Christmas celebrations. Eventually, they had to say their goodbyes to all the friends they had made throughout the year.

Their teacher told them to write and tell the class about their new school in New York.

It was the last Saturday before Christmas and Dad said, "Let's go and get our Christmas tree from the market." They all walked up to Petticoat Lane, but the market traders had all sold out. Then, one man from one of the stalls said, "It has been so hectic but I can tell you where you can go and select your own."

So, it was back to get the car and off they went. The man's directions took them out of town and into the countryside. They had to find a Christmas tree farm in Holly Lane.

They drove for ages but seemed to be driving round in circles. Then, all of a sudden, Dad stopped the car and wound down his window. There, outside a little cottage, stood an old man. Dad asked him for directions to the Christmas tree farm. The old man replied, "Down the lane and follow the shadow."

Matt and Molly looked at each other and Matt shouted to the man, "What shadow?"

The old man replied, "It's the shadow from the Christmas trees. They're all along the side of the lane, then at the end you will find Mr. and Mrs. Christmas. They will sort you out a tree."

When they arrived at the farm, an old man was just about to shut the gate. Dad said, "Excuse me. We have come a long way. Do you have any trees left?"

Mr. Christmas said, "You are lucky. We have one

left. It must have your name on it!"

Matt went over and had a look but could not see a name. The old man said, "No, it's just a saying."

They wrapped the tree in hessian, tied it to the roof rack and Dad then paid Mr. Christmas.

Matt and Molly were just getting into the car when they spotted *The Shadow* floating in and out of the Christmas trees in the woods.

The Shadow shouted to Matt and Molly, "How do you think I am doing with my shadow dancing?"

He then jumped up onto the roof of the car and Molly said, "You will have to hold on tight."

When they arrived back home, Dad carried the tree into the lounge and stood it up in the front bay window, looking out into the square.

Matt and Molly helped put up the decorations and the lights looked spectacular.

After tea, they all went out into the square to admire the tree all lit up. It was so magical for Matt and Molly and then all around Nightingale Square, their neighbours switched their lights on, one by one.

The Shadow whispered into Molly's ear, "I haven't seen the square lit up like this since 1949."

That night, when they went to bed, *The Shadow* popped in and said, "Tomorrow is Christmas Eve and I believe it is a very special day."

"Yes," beamed Matt and Molly, "it is our birthday. What special treat do you have for us?"

Bertie replied, "It is the last code, so open the book and read what it says."

NUMBERS WILL TAKE YOU TO THIS DOOR

Down this street

A shadow you might meet.

Horse and guards will help you get there

But remember Parliament Square.

You can ask questions

Only if you dare

But remember

It's not Mr. Blair

HORSE/BLACK DOOR/2X5/ GUARDS/STREET

The Shadow asked them, "What do you think?" Matt and Molly looked at him, shrugged their shoulders and said, "We don't have a clue."

Then Matt asked, "Who is Mr. Blair?" *The Shadow* replied, "A lot of people ask that question, so you two have sweet dreams about the questions you could ask."

The next morning Matt and Molly woke really early and when they walked into the dining room they saw that the table was loaded with presents and cards. Mum and Dad were having coffee in the snug and shouted out, "Happy birthday to you both," as they joined them in the dining room.

Matt and Molly opened their cards and presents. They both had watches and books, and Mum said, "Tonight you have your big surprise but you'll have to wait till then." They were so excited they thanked Mum and Dad and ran upstairs to look at their presents.

The Shadow popped in and said, "We haven't got time for that, even though you have got new watches. Come on! We have the last code to find."

Matt and Molly ran downstairs and put on their hats and coats and told Mum they were going to see the Beefeaters at the Tower and feed the birds one last time. Dad called out, "Don't forget, we have a surprise tonight!"

The Shadow followed them out of the door and ran past them shouting, "I will beat you to Parliament Square," and disappeared into the distance.

Matt said, "Come on, Molly. I think it is a bus trip."
The old Routemaster stopped and on they jumped.
They asked the bus conductor for two tickets to
Parliament Square. Matt and Molly ran up the
stairs to the front of the bus. The twins could see
The Shadow floating down the street, then, the traffic
lights changed to red and the bus came to a halt
but Bertie kept drifting in and out of the traffic until
he was out of sight.

By the time Matt and Molly reached Trafalgar
Square, *The Shadow* had been there for ten minutes
or more. The twins jumped off the bus and Matt
said, "Right, we are looking for the first code. Here
we go."

As they were walking down Whitehall the road got
wider and wider, then Matt saw some **GUARDs**
riding **HORSES** and said, "That's two of the
codes."

"Yes, you are right," replied Molly. Matt and Molly
carried on walking and then, in front of them, they
could see a large stone statue like a tall tower in
the centre of the road. All around the tower, people
had laid wreaths made up of poppies. This was
the Cenotaph and on it was a plaque with names
inscribed in the stone of men and woman who had
lost their lives in the wars from the past. Matt said,
"They must have been special people to have such
a beautiful statue and, as the words say, they will
never be forgotten."

As Matt and Molly stood there, a bell rang out across the road and, as they turned, they could see soldiers with tall furry black hats marching.

There was a large crowd of people watching and taking pictures standing next to the soldiers who stood so still they could have been a mime. Suddenly, a lady at the front of the crowd said, "Right, we have seen the changing of the guards. Now, the next stop is the Prime Minister's house, No 10."

Matt looked at the code breaker book and pointed out to Molly, "Look **2** **x** **5** equals 10. It's another code."

Matt and Molly followed a group of people who were being shown around London by a tour guide. After a short walk they arrived at some very large gates where a policeman was standing **GUARD**.

Matt said, "That is number four off the list." As they looked through the gates, they could see the road sign. It read Downing **STREET**. Molly said, "Fifth code. One to go and I wonder whether the Prime Minister is at home."

Matt looked up at the roof and said, "I can't see any flags flying; he can't be at home." All of a sudden, the policeman on duty asked the crowd to stand back. The gates slowly opened and a black car with tinted windows drove into Downing Street. There were reporters standing in the corner with their cameras all waiting for the best picture. The car doors opened and one of the reporters shouted out, "Will the Shadow Minister be sacked?" The Prime Minister bowed his head tapped his cane and said, "The Shadow Minister will never leave Old London Town."

Matt said to Molly, "That makes two of them!" and then the Prime Minister walked up to the front door, which had been opened from the inside and, as it shut, Molly said, "Look, it is the BLACK DOOR and it's No. 10." They had broken the last and final code, without even a calculator!

On the way home they thought about all the good times they had had and how hard it was going to be to say goodbye to The Shadow, who had kept them safe and sound through all their adventures in Old London Town.

When they arrived home The Shadow was sitting on the steps waiting for their return. He said, "Well, you have cracked the last code and you are the only children to have completed the code breaker book. HAPPY BIRTHDAY."

Bertie handed them both a present. They unwrapped the packages and inside each was a long cane, just like his.

He told them to unscrew the handle and, as they did, inside was a code breaker game which you play with the help of dice, which were also inside the cane.

Matt and Molly were thrilled and thanked Bertie for their presents which they would treasure forever.

The twins walked into the hallway and Dad said, "Have you had a good birthday?"

"Yes," they both replied.

Dad told them to go upstairs and get washed and changed.

When they came back down Mum called, "In here." Matt and Molly walked through into the lounge and there was a loud cheer of happy birthday greetings from Mum, Dad, Grandma, Grandpa, Aunt Laura and Uncle Frank. On the table were their presents and birthday cards and a large cake in the shape of a hat and cane, with nine candles on each side. Mum said, "I got the inspiration by the ones on the stand!"

Matt and Molly had a lovely birthday with their family and Christmas Day was even better, but they knew the day after Boxing Day they would have to start packing their cases ready to leave.

On Boxing Day everyone went next door for a drink and to say their final goodbyes.

That night *The Shadow* went in to see Matt and Molly and said, "I know by tomorrow morning you will be packed and ready to go but I must ask for the code breaker book. Matt told him that it was in his case already packed. *The Shadow* shook his head and said, "I'm sorry, you cannot take it with you. It must be put back in the place where you found it, so when the next children arrive they too will be able to play the code breaker game, just like the ones before them over the last hundred years or more."

Matt and Molly took the book back to the attic and put it back in the box and shut the door.

Molly came back downstairs to her room and she finished off the last chapter of their new book and Matt came in and fitted his pictures into the manuscript. They put it in a jiffy bag and took it to their Mum's agent George who lived just round the corner.

That night Matt and Molly could not sleep, thinking that this was their last night in the house.

Eventually, the dreaded morning arrived and they could hear the removal men outside talking.

They spent all morning loading the lorry, furniture first, then all the boxes.

Matt and Molly were in the snug when they heard Mum's phone ring. It was George, her literary agent. He said, "Yes, yes, yes, the new book is amazing." She could not understand what he was talking about but asked him to give her five minutes and she would pop round to see him.

George showed her the manuscript and she said, "That's Molly's writing and the only one in the family who can draw like that is Matt." George said, "I think this one will be a best seller." Mum told him to carry on and have it published but not to say anything to the children for the moment.

"O.K.," agreed George, "I will keep you informed."

Mum went back home but never said a word to Matt and Molly. Their car was packed with the cases and ready to go. The family were going on a cruise liner and they had a long journey ahead to the docks at Southampton.

Matt and Molly searched the house from top to bottom but could not find *The Shadow* anywhere, but his hat and cane were still on the stand, so he must have been around somewhere. They just wanted to say one last goodbye, but perhaps that was not to be.

Dad called out, "Come on, kids, into the car and I will lock the door." Dad looked around the hall one more time, then closed the door and turned the key. Mum shouted, "You can put that hat and cane back."

Dad shrugged his shoulders, opened the door once

again and put them back on the stand.

Matt and Molly were in the car looking at the house as Dad drove off.

Matt and Molly turned in their seat and looked back for one more glimpse and there, at the front door stood *The Shadow*, and, for the very first time, they saw his wife standing by his side.

The Shadow gave a wave and a tear dropped from his eye but never reached the floor.

Matt and Molly also had tears in their eyes, blew him a kiss and waved till the house was out of sight.

THE END

Tap tap tap .....

THE SHADOW OF OLD LONDON TOWN

Matt and Molly's book became a best seller and was sold all over Old London Town - by barrow boys and girls and from Harrods to Clink Jail. Now that you have this book, you will have to listen out for the tap tap tap, and you will have fun without a shadow of doubt.

Matt and Molly

"An amazing read without a shadow of a doubt
From your friend Bertie"..........